Dragon Mage 1: Promise

Dragon Mage 1: Promise

Avril Sabine

Cracked Acorn Productions
Australia

Dragon Mage 1: Promise

Published by

Cracked Acorn Productions

PO Box 1365

Gympie, Queensland 4570

Australia

978-1-925941-11-1 (Kindle)

978-1-925941-12-8 (EPUB)

978-1-925941-13-5 (Print)

Genre: Young Adult Urban Fantasy

Copyright 2020 © Avril Sabine

Cover design by Caitlyn Petersen

*For all those who asked for more stories about
Amber, Kade and Ronan. I listened. Enjoy.*

Ronan is adamant that Amber owes him and expects her to repay him by tracking someone down. Amber soon finds that, as always, when dealing with dragons, nothing is simple. Surrounded by enemies, and without her usual allies, Amber needs to find a way out of danger and discover how to return home before it's too late and she's stuck in a world far from her own.

*

This story was written by an Australian author using Australian spelling.

Name Pronunciation

Like many names there is more than one way to pronounce the following ones. These are the pronunciations used in this story.

Anja (ann-jah)

Becan (beck-ann)

Brigitte (brish-eet)

Caral (care-al)

Cort (rhymes with caught)

Daray (dah-ray)

Devona (de-vone-ah)

Edvin (ed-vin)

Jorn (rhymes with thorn)

Gilda (gil-dah)

Gunsa (gun-suh)

Gwynham (gwin-hem)

Hella (hel-la)

Keeley (keel-ee)

Maira (may-rah)

Morgane (more-gain)

Ninian (nin-ee-an)

Paili (pah-lee)

Rian (ree-in)

Ronan (row-nen)

Runa (roo-nah)

Shylah (shy-luh)

Starne (star-n)

Tahmid (tar-mid)

Tanith (tan-ith)

Tathen (tath-en)

Treon (tree-on)

Other pronunciations:

Pliethin (plea-thin)

Temolae Keep (tem-oh-lay)

Chapter One

Amber half sat up in bed when someone stepped out of the Void, dropping back onto her pillow when she realised it was Ronan. Beside her, Kade had become human.

"Don't even think about going back to sleep," Ronan warned. "Get out of bed."

"It's the middle of the night," Amber protested. She had no idea what time it was, but the room was dark so it certainly wasn't morning. And absolutely not time to get up. She was tempted to roll onto her side and ignore him. But no one ignored Ronan. Not if they were smart.

Ronan stepped forward and grabbed her arm, tugging her out of bed. "I need you to find someone for me."

Stumbling, Amber started to protest, but doubted Ronan would listen. What was he doing awake at this hour? He'd joined them at each location the past three days when Hell Hounds had entered their world, helping them take the Hell Hounds to where they could fight them without causing worldwide panic. Didn't he ever rest? Bloody dragon. She glared at him, trying to come up with a way to convince him to let her sleep. Nothing came to mind.

"You owe me," Ronan warned.

Amber pulled out of his grip. She wasn't about to let him get away with that. Raising her chin, she met his gaze. "We're even. You agreed we'd be even when we finished with Tahmid." She tried not to think about the day she'd killed that particular dragon.

"You owe me for killing Martin. Are you trying to tell me you didn't take him to the crypt for me to kill?" Ronan demanded.

Amber glanced at Kade who remained in bed, watching them. She sighed heavily. So much for sleeping in and having a lazy Saturday. She should have expected something would ruin that plan. Although she would have preferred a call from the Hell Hound emergency line than whatever Ronan had in mind. Facing a dozen Hell Hounds was likely to be easier. "This will make us even? Whatever you've planned."

Ronan's predatory smile formed. "That will depend on if you can track down the one I'm looking for."

"Do you have something I can use?" She supposed she should get it over and done with. She grabbed a shirt out of the chest of drawers to throw over her dragon-leather vest that was the same deep brown as her trousers.

"I would have demanded you repay what you owed me months ago if it hadn't taken me so long to get what was needed."

Kade sat up in bed, his gaze on Amber who drew on her wrist sheaths that each contained a dagger, pushing her power filled bracelets out of the way, having already put on her boots, belt and sword. "If you're back in time for breakfast, we could still have that picnic we were thinking of going on."

"If she would stop messing around, we might have a chance of being back by then." Ronan grabbed Amber's hand before she could collect the caged Pliethin that hung from the curtain rod and took her through the Void to a cave, remaining in the Void. She wanted to protest being unable to collect the caged Pliethin or her phone. She also wanted to pull away from his grip, but remained where she was since she didn't want to get stuck in the Void. She had no idea what would happen if she was stuck, but since no one had ever returned, she doubted it'd be good. "Where are we?"

"That doesn't matter." Ronan took a lock of hair and a small, jagged rock from his pocket. He held them out to Amber. "I need to find the woman this hair is from and the rock is from the place where she was taken before the first binding was done."

She stared at the lock that was a mixture of rich brown and gold strands, not taking the objects. "Which one did you have trouble finding?" It seemed odd to think of Ronan holding onto a lock of hair. He wasn't the sentimental type.

Ronan didn't answer immediately. "The rock."

She met his gaze, staring into his gold eyes. He wanted her to find someone from his past? Someone whose lock of hair he'd kept for centuries? "Who is she?"

"Someone I made a promise to a very long time ago."

She should have known by now how impossible it was to get information out of Ronan. And asking him if the woman had been his lover certainly wouldn't encourage him to answer. "Why here?" Ronan always had a reason for everything he did. Even if it was only to cause trouble or piss someone off.

"I already told you. That isn't important."

"Of course it's important otherwise you wouldn't have brought me here."

"I thought you were in a hurry."

Amber grinned. "Anyone would think you were trying to avoid talking about some sad love story."

Ronan's eyes narrowed. "Just because we were once lovers, it doesn't mean I've spent all these centuries pining away for her. I promised her that one day I'd find a way to take her back to her home. I always keep my promises. Don't I, kitten?"

She wasn't sure if she should continue to push him with the threatening tone of his last three words. But he did have a tendency not to tell her vital information. "Then why here?"

"This is where he found us. It's the last place where she was in this world, before she was taken to another."

Still meeting Ronan's gaze, she took the items from him. "What is her name?"

"Brigitte."

With a nod, she closed her hand on the items, trying to sense where the location was. She wouldn't be able to find Brigitte until she was in the same world as her. Not that it was a guarantee. She was still learning how to track down locations and people. Her eyes opened as a thought occurred to her.

"What is wrong?" Ronan demanded.

She wished there was something else she could say, but she wasn't about to start lying to Ronan. That'd be a terrible idea. "What if she's dead?" She studied him, trying to tell if her words bothered him.

"Then I return her remains to her home."

"Okay." She closed her eyes again. Obviously he wasn't pining away for the love of his life. Surely even Ronan would have shown some sort of emotion at that thought if he was. Although it was Ronan.

"How long is this going to take?"

Again she opened her eyes. "A lot less time if I'm not constantly interrupted."

"Get on with it," Ronan growled.

She almost pointed out that he'd been the one to interrupt her. She kept her mouth closed. Somehow. Breathing out heavily, she focused on the rock. There was a tug and she followed it, drawing it towards her, sensing another world. "I found it." Opening her eyes, she grinned at Ronan. "I've got it if you want to take us there."

Ronan shifted them through the Void, once again remaining in it when they reached the next destination.

Amber scanned the area. They were in a lush forest. The place seemed to be empty. No buildings, no structures of any sort, only trees. They could be anywhere.

"Where to now?" Ronan demanded.

From the Void she could only sense the threads, or pathways as the dragons liked to call them, of her world, the Dragons' world and the Hell Hounds' world. She had no threads for this place. Not that she would have been able to travel to them even if she had any since Ronan hadn't given her the chance to collect her caged Pliethin. "You'll have to take me out of the Void. I can't sense anyone or anything from here."

Ronan took them out of the Void before he let go of her. "Any other orders while you're at it?"

Her sense of the place crashed in on her and she grabbed his arm. The crisp, clean smell of the forest washed over her. The soft sounds of the wind in the trees and the low noises of the creatures were all that she heard. But they weren't all that she sensed. "Take us back in."

He didn't hesitate, shifting them to the Void. "Now what?"

"We were surrounded."

"Impossible. All I could smell was animals and I know you can't see into the Void like Crystal."

"I couldn't smell them either, or hear them, but I

could sense them. There were easily a dozen of them, travelling through the forest in pairs. The moment we appeared, they started moving towards us."

Ronan took her hand before forcing his way through the Void. "They were human?"

"Maybe. Although I suppose they could have been dragons in human form." She hated trying to move through the Void. It felt like trying to walk through deep water.

"What can you tell me then?" Ronan demanded.

She almost pointed out that he was the one who'd demanded her help, not the other way around. "They were headed in the other direction before they noticed us come out of the Void."

"Then we leave the area and they should continue with whatever plans they had."

"I thought this wasn't going to take long," Amber muttered.

"You're the one slowing us down." Ronan continued to force his way through the Void.

Amber opened her mouth, closing it again. It was pointless commenting. She should have known it would take a lot longer than Ronan had insinuated. Bloody dragon. Always complicating things. She tried to focus on finding the owner of the lock of hair.

It was impossible. She really needed to be out of the Void to find her. "Is she as old as you?"

Ronan glanced over his shoulder, continuing to tug her along. "Who?"

"The woman you want me to track down." It took her a moment to think of the name. "Brigitte."

"No."

"But she is pretty old, isn't she?" Amber persisted. "I mean, she'd have to be. The worlds were bound together centuries ago." The moment she'd spoken the words, she realised she'd also told Ronan that he was old. Hopefully he didn't take that as an insult.

"How far from us were the ones who were hidden?"

Amber shrugged. "I don't know. A few metres. Maybe more."

"For someone concerned with how long this will take, you're not trying very hard."

Her relief hadn't lasted long. He was obviously annoyed about something. "And maybe you should have given me more information so I would have been better prepared."

Ronan stopped and faced her, keeping hold of her hand. "The moment I come out of the Void, I'll shift. You climb onto my back and I'll fly away from here.

You should be able to find Brigitte while we're in the air."

"A pity you didn't bring a saddle."

"Are you ready?" Ronan demanded.

Amber grinned. As if she'd be stupid enough to say no when he used that tone of voice. "Of course I'm ready."

"You better be." Ronan had barely finished speaking when he took them out of the Void.

Amber sensed the people nearby, all of them again moving in their direction. The moment Ronan became a dragon she clambered onto his back. "Fly. Now."

Ronan launched into the air. *"How many of them are there?"*

She counted them, mentally tracking their movements. "Twelve. And they're running in our direction." She peered down below. "I still can't see, hear or smell them. There's something seriously wrong with this place."

"Are you certain they're human?"

She mentally searched for them again. They were too far from the location now. "I have no idea. They seemed human, but I guess that doesn't mean much." She glanced over her shoulder, frowning. There had been something about them that she'd recognised, but she couldn't figure it out. "They were only moving as fast as a human. We've left them behind."

"Tell me if you notice any others."

Not wanting to stay in this world any longer than she had to, Amber focused on finding the owner of the lock of hair. She'd nearly given up, beginning to think they were in a different world or too far from her to find, when she felt a tug in the direction of the mountains. "Are they snow-capped?"

"How about focusing on the task instead of worrying about everything else," Ronan said.

"I am focusing on the task. We have to go towards the mountains off to our right. Are they snow-capped? Because if they are, I'm not dressed for cold climates." She was already cold enough flying so high above the ground. "We should go home and get some gear."

Ronan veered towards the right. *"Stop trying to come up with excuses to get out of helping me."*

"It makes sense. You seriously can't expect me to go to the snow with you dressed like this."

"All I need to do is collect Brigitte and return home. I'm not planning on taking a holiday."

She could hear the underlying annoyance in his words. "Do you even know what a holiday is? Or are you always too busy plotting and planning to take time out for something as ordinary as a holiday?"

"No reason why one means you can't do the other."

Chapter Two

Amber grinned, even though he still sounded annoyed. He probably plotted in his sleep. Her grin faded as the air grew colder and she leaned forward to press herself against him. "It'll only take a few minutes to go home and get warmer clothes. I could also collect a caged Pliethin." It felt odd not having one hanging at her side.

"Then there'll be something else. Then one more thing. I promised to take her home as soon as it was possible. Which is now. We're not leaving until we find her."

Amber shivered and her breath frosted on the air. "So I'll end up with frostbite or something just so you can keep your promise. What about your promise to me?"

"Change form. Your goshawk should handle this weather better than your human form."

She sat up to glare at Ronan even though he

couldn't see it. He always had to be difficult. Why couldn't he take her home? "You need to go more to the right. We're getting closer." The cold air felt like it sliced through her.

It wasn't long before a castle came into view, clinging to the side of the mountain, ground access only on one side. Ronan headed straight for it, slowing slightly. *"Are you sure this is the location? I can smell wyverns."*

"Positive. She's outside the castle. On the side with the sheer drop." Amber wrapped her arms around herself, her legs tightening around him so she didn't fall. It was ridiculously cold. Ronan better be right in that they wouldn't be staying long. Her teeth were starting to chatter. "There. See her? She's walking with two men." Amber frowned. "I can smell wyverns too. And sense them. I could swear it's coming from the two men." She scanned the area below, noticing there were numerous hidden people scattered around the castle, always in pairs.

The three people below turned to face them as Ronan swooped down out of the sky, landing on the ground and becoming human the moment Amber was off his back. "Brigitte." He took a single step towards her.

Amber remained where she was, surprised Ronan

wasn't hiding what he looked like, but she supposed Brigitte had known him back when he'd looked like himself. He was a little shorter than usual, more muscular and looked far too young. His hair was a white blond, but the colour of his eyes remained gold. She was surprised he didn't make himself appear taller like he normally did with how the two males towered over him, their tense figures and wild look in their eyes making them seem like they might pick a fight just for the fun of it.

"Ronan?" Brigitte took a step towards him, waving the two men back. "How did you get here? I'd given up on you coming for me centuries ago."

"I had to wait until the binding of the worlds had been broken." Ronan's predatory smile made a brief appearance. "It would have taken a few more decades if I hadn't hurried the process along."

Brigitte closed the distance between them, placing her hand against his cheek. "You didn't have gold eyes back when I knew you." She smiled up at him.

Amber wanted to warn Ronan against the woman, but doubted he'd want her to interfere. There was something about the way Brigitte smiled that made Amber wary.

Ronan captured Brigitte's hand, holding it between

both of his. "There were a few things I kept to myself."

Amber barely managed not to tell him to hurry. She was freezing. They were more sheltered behind the walls surrounding the castle, but it didn't help much. She kept her arms wrapped around herself, her teeth chattering. Couldn't he save his almost lies for later? After they'd taken Brigitte home.

"Your companion is cold. We should go inside and talk." Brigitte started to turn away, her hand remaining in Ronan's.

He drew her back to him. "I'm here to keep my promise of taking you back to your home."

"Come inside first," Brigitte insisted. She smiled again, trying to draw him towards her. The smile faded. "Come with me, Ronan."

Ronan didn't move. "I have other plans for the day. Do you still wish me to take you home?"

Brigitte took a step towards Ronan. "There are things that need to be done first."

Amber also took a step closer to Ronan, planning to suggest they take Brigitte up on her offer of going inside. Hopefully, there'd be a fireplace with a fire burning in it and she'd have the chance to thaw out. Brigitte spoke before she could.

"Surely you understand I can't leave on such short

notice." Brigitte again tried to tug Ronan towards the castle.

He didn't budge. "We can set a day for me to return and I'll take you back then."

Brigitte inclined her head. "That makes a great deal of sense." She smiled up at him. "Before you go, let me give you a gift to show you how grateful I am that you've finally arrived." She undid the bracelet that was on her wrist, a solid metal that was grey in colour and hinged so it snapped open.

"That isn't necessary."

Brigitte snapped the bracelet closed, pressing her lips to it before raising her head to smile up at him again. "A Gold dragon is exactly what I need."

Amber didn't like the way the woman eyed Ronan. A shiver ran through her as she thought of how many centuries of practice Brigitte had at plotting and planning. And the shiver wasn't because of the cold. She no longer wanted to go inside where she could get warm. All she wanted to do was leave. "Ronan-" She broke off when a woman swooped down to land beside Ronan. She had dragon wings with gold veins. They sank into her back, her dragon-leather, long sleeve shirt smooth and unbroken where they'd been.

The woman dragged Ronan away from Brigitte.

"Gwynham? No. Impossible. Brigitte killed him." She slowly shook her head. "But you're so much like him. Except for your eyes. They're gold when his was blue shot through with gold. Who are you?" The woman turned to Brigitte, not giving Ronan time to answer. "Is this why you demanded I meet with you? What trick are you planning? Or are you trying to tell me I missed one of them? I know he's not Gwynham. What cruel trick are you trying to play this time?"

"Who are you?" Ronan demanded, interrupting Brigitte who'd started to speak. "And who is Gwynham?" He took a step back from the woman.

"Gwynham was my twin." Morgane glanced at Brigitte before returning her attention to Ronan. "And Brigitte is my mother." Her words were flat, containing none of her initial emotions.

Amber looked from one to the other, pretty certain she wasn't just Brigitte's daughter. Especially with her white blond hair that was the same colour as Ronan's. Her eyes were different though, the brown of them flecked with gold, closer to the almost gold colour of Brigitte's eyes. "I'm guessing she's your daughter." She looked at Ronan, his expression unreadable, before she returned her attention to the women, not trusting either of them.

Brigitte gave Amber a dismissive glance before

returning her attention to the other woman. "How thoughtful of you to visit me, Morgane. I'd begun to think you wouldn't turn up."

"Is it true?" Ronan demanded. "Is she my daughter?"

"I'll have my people show you inside, Ronan. You can't expect to turn up here without notice and have me drop everything to deal with you. Especially not after all this time." Brigitte waved one of the men forward. "We'll talk shortly."

Ronan gave the man a look that would deter most people. The man kept coming towards him, grabbing his arm when he was close enough. "If your man would keep his arm, you'd best tell him to unhand me, Brigitte."

Morgane continued to study Ronan. "I want to know if it's true as well. Is this man my father?"

"You don't have a father," Brigitte snapped. She turned to Ronan. "And you will harm none of my people."

"Then tell him to unhand me."

Amber tried to speak mind to mind with Ronan, but it was like he wasn't there. Surely he wouldn't be blocking her. "Ronan." She remained where she was when she would have preferred to move even closer.

They needed to get out of here. "I need to speak to you."

Ronan's gaze remained on Brigitte, ignoring the man who held his arm. "What have you done to me?"

"You weren't expecting to find the same girl you deserted, were you Ronan?"

Ronan's predatory smile formed. "I never deserted you and you're not the only one who's changed. Did you think you would be?"

"Is he my father?" Morgane looked from one to the other. "Is he?"

"How many times do I have to tell you that you don't have a father? Now where are those you never seem to be away from?"

"You told me to come alone."

"Since when have you listened to me?" Brigitte asked.

"Why can't I shift forms or mind speak?" Ronan demanded.

Again Amber tried to reach him mentally, hoping that if both of them were trying it would make a difference. She kept her arms wrapped around herself, shivering in the frigid air. If they didn't get out of here soon she was likely to have frostbite.

"Answer me, Brigitte," Ronan said. "What have you done to me?"

Morgane glanced at Ronan. "It's the bracelet. It keeps you in your human form. She's improved on the original version so you might as well be human. Without the word used to bind it, you won't be able to remove it."

Amber looked from the bracelet Morgane wore to the one Ronan had around his wrist. "Is that why you can't completely change shape?" She moved closer to Ronan even though it meant moving closer to Brigitte and her warriors. If things went bad, or at least worse than they already were, she'd need to protect him. He didn't know what it was like to be human.

Morgane smiled. "No. My bracelet was one of Brigitte's early failures."

"It wasn't the bracelet that was the failure." Brigitte looked pointedly at Morgane.

"Then maybe you should have put in some effort instead of raising us for our hearts." Morgane's words were light, the look in her eyes anything but.

Amber stared at Brigitte. "You deliberately killed your son for his heart?" Had she found someone more ruthless than Ronan?

Brigitte shrugged. "When you're dumped in a world without Gold dragons, you do the best you can."

"You killed my son for his heart?" Ronan demanded.

"He was my son. I've already said he didn't have a father," Brigitte stated.

"If you aren't interested in telling me why you wanted to meet with me, then it's probably past time I left." Morgane's wings formed, stretching out behind her.

Brigitte grabbed hold of Morgane's arm. "I did not give you permission to leave."

Morgane tried to pull away from Brigitte. Her mother refused to let go.

"Remove this bracelet from me," Ronan demanded. Neither of them paid him any attention, both glaring at each other, Brigitte's man continuing to hold Ronan's arm.

Sensing numerous dragons and riders flying in fast, Amber grabbed Ronan's arm and drew him away from Morgane and Brigitte. She glared at the warrior who came with him. "We're surrounded." She started to say by dragons and riders, but frowned instead. "I could almost believe they were wyverns."

"My people have orders to set fire to your villages and the crops if you detain me," Morgane said.

"I doubt you have it in you to do that." Brigitte's

lips twisted into a smile. "I knew you'd bring them with you."

Amber continued to tug Ronan away from the women, wishing the man would let him go. She kept her voice low, knowing that the dragons were likely to hear her anyway. "We have to leave."

"Neither of you are to go anywhere," Brigitte said. "I haven't finished with either of you."

Amber sensed the hidden warriors before they swooped down on them, changing into a panther and launching herself at the one that tried to grab her. She snarled when another tried to attack her, realising she was right. They were wyverns. Yet their minds didn't feel like those of wyverns and they blocked her from reading their thoughts. When more of them focused on her, she changed into a goshawk and flew into the sky. Several followed. Below she saw that Ronan was pinned to the ground and Morgane struggled to escape from Brigitte. There was no way she could rescue Ronan on her own. They were completely outnumbered and he might as well be human.

Amber flew at Brigitte's face. The woman shielded her eyes, letting Morgane go. Before Brigitte could grab hold of Morgane, she flew into the sky. Amber flew upwards out of Brigitte's reach. She scanned the area, looking for Ronan. He was gone. For a second, she feared the bracelet prevented her from finding him.

She angled out of the way of Brigitte, who'd shifted into her dragon form, flying above the castle. Ronan was inside. Somewhere deep within. And she doubted he'd gone willingly. She dodged Brigitte's claws, crying out as she angled away from the castle, trying to keep it in sight as she searched for a way inside. All the windows she could see were closed. She didn't blame them in this weather.

Again she dodged Brigitte's attack, blocking when the woman tried to talk to her in her mind. There was no way she could rescue Ronan on her own and she certainly wasn't about to trust anything Brigitte had to say. What sort of person had kids so she could eat their hearts? The woman made Ronan look like a saint in comparison. And that was saying something.

Chapter Three

Hating the need to leave Ronan behind, she headed away from Brigitte and the castle, flying after Morgane. The enemy of her enemy might make a good ally. If she'd been in human form, she would have been slowly shaking her head. She'd obviously been around Ronan far too long to be thinking like that. Yet what else could she do? Fear threatened to swamp her. She focused on the facts, trying not to think of all the things that might go wrong.

She was in a strange land, the only person she knew had been captured and the only thing she had was the clothes and weapons she wore, her power filled bracelets and her power filled jewellery. A pendant and an earring. And her skills. It wasn't much. If she wanted to survive, then Ronan was probably the person to emulate.

Sensing that Brigitte continued to follow, no

longer trying to force her way into her mind, she put on a burst of speed. How long would the dragon follow? Well behind Brigitte were the warriors that reminded Amber of wyverns. What sort of strange place was this? She really hoped she wasn't stuck here long enough to find out. If she could convince Morgane to create a distraction, she could sneak in and rescue Ronan and they could get the hell out of here. Surely being captured by Brigitte meant he no longer needed to keep his promise to her.

As they left the mountains behind, and the air grew slightly warmer, Brigitte and her warriors turned away, heading back towards the castle. Amber noticed two dragons and riders join them as they reached the edge of a forest, none of them visible. She had no idea if they were friend or foe. She reached for Morgane's mind, hoping she didn't block her.

"Why do you follow me? If you think I can convince Brigitte to let your companion go just because she gave birth to me, then you're very much mistaken."

"Do you know there are two dragons and their riders following us?" She currently had nothing to bargain with so there was no point asking for help yet. Dragons rarely did anything unless there was a benefit in it for them. At least most dragons didn't.

Morgane slowed so Amber could come alongside

her. When she was close, she spoke aloud. "How do you know there are two dragons and their riders nearby?"

"I can sense them." Before she could ask why Morgane had spoken aloud, the woman spoke again.

"Impossible. No one can sense a hunter when they use magic to bend the light around themselves. Especially not a hunter with centuries of experience."

"Is that what the people riding dragons are called?" Amber followed Morgane to the ground.

As soon as Morgane's feet touched the grass of the forest clearing, her wings drew back in until they were once more a part of her body. "What are you?"

Amber landed in front of Morgane, becoming human. She wasn't sure it was a good idea to have become human when the dragons and their riders landed one on either side of Morgane, remaining hidden. "I'm a Dragon Mage. I take it the dragons and the hunters who landed on either side of you are your people."

Morgane made a gesture and the four of them became visible. "Can you see all hunters that are hiding?"

Amber glanced at the dragons and hunters. Both hunters had similar colouring. Dark brown hair and eyes. One of them also had a close-cropped beard that circled his mouth and chin, going along his jawline. She wished she could say yes with how interested Morgane seemed in her answer. She shook her head. "Sensing is different to seeing. I could be blindfolded and still tell you how many are here and where they are."

The hunter with the close-cropped beard dismounted and came to stand beside Morgane, slipping an arm around her waist. "This might be the advantage we've been looking for. We can't continue to run."

"What would you have us do, Jorn? Give her our Golds? Who would you sacrifice? One of our own or would you expect another to give their life to appease Brigitte's greed? And I refuse to stay in one of the towns or villages of your people and bring her hybrid army down on them. The castle couldn't withstand an attack from her hybrids. How could a town or village?" Morgane demanded.

Jorn faced Morgane, his hand that had been resting against her back now on her hip. "You can stay behind. None would think badly of you if you didn't fight this battle. It's past time to do what we should have done centuries ago."

Morgane sighed. "She went into the mountains

with nothing. Only a handful of people. No one could have expected her to create an army."

"I'm not blaming you," Jorn said softly. "None of us expected it."

There were so many things Amber wanted to know, but she was pretty certain the two in front of her wouldn't answer her questions. But she hoped they'd clarify one thing for her. "Why do Brigitte's warriors seem like wyverns? When I sense them, it's like I'm sensing a wyvern. Even when they're hidden."

The hunter who'd remained on the dragon studied Amber. "Can anyone learn how to sense those who are hidden like you can? That would have been a useful skill to have last time I explored our world."

She was tempted to trade the information, but she needed them more than they needed her. "It's one of the abilities I gained when I became a Dragon Mage. There's no guarantee it will be the ability gained when someone becomes one. It seems to be one of the less common abilities."

The hunter slipped off the dragon. "So what you're telling us is that if we want access to an ability like yours, then you're the only one with it."

"As far as I know I'm the only one in this world who has the ability." Amber tried to contain her excitement. It looked like she had something to bargain with after all.

The dragon the second hunter had been riding became human. "Are you insane, Cort? I'm not about to let your thirst for adventure put the rest of our people in danger. Haven't we already lost enough? Would you have the rest of us die as-" He broke off, glancing at Morgane and giving her a nod.

As much as Amber liked being able to talk mind to mind, it had its downsides. Like when other people used the ability and she was left in the dark as to what was going on. "Does Brigitte need to be killed, or will taking her back to the world she came from be enough? That's why Ronan and I came here. To keep his promise to her now the binding between all the worlds has been broken."

"He's Gold," Morgane said. "If you're hoping he'll still be alive, you might want to ready yourself for a disappointment. Brigitte won't care whose heart she takes. All that is important is that it's gold and it will prevent her from ageing."

Amber couldn't resist smiling, one she was pretty certain was similar to Ronan's predatory smile. "I have every faith in your father's ability to survive no matter the odds."

The other dragon became human and all four of

Morgane's companions fired questions at her, speaking over each other.

Morgane held up a hand, silence forming. She met Amber's gaze. "Did you not hear Brigitte? I have no father."

Amber laughed. "It's probably better that way with how much of a bastard Ronan can be." Although he had his moments when she could believe he cared about something other than his own survival.

Morgane studied Amber. "Is that why you left him behind?"

"No." Amber met Morgane's gaze. "I will go after him. He's my ally." She smiled. "You might call him family. And I never desert family."

Morgane and Jorn shared a look, Jorn giving her a nod. Morgane turned to Amber. "I need to know if you can sense any hunter who is using their magic to bend the light around them and hide their scent and sounds."

Amber shrugged. "I don't know for certain if I can, but I could sense ones hidden in the forest before we headed towards the castle." She frowned. "Now I think of it, they were like the warriors at the castle. They reminded me of wyverns. I didn't realise what they reminded me of at the time. Only that it was familiar."

"Where in the forest?" The second dragon stepped close to Amber, grabbing her shoulder. "Which direction?"

Meeting his gaze, she refused to back down. "How about you ask nicely?"

Jorn tugged the dragon away from Amber. "Tathen." When the dragon took a step back from Amber, he turned to her. "Our people are hiding in the forest. The only hybrids in existence are Brigitte's. No one else was insane enough to breed with wyverns. Nor would they even if they could get hold of her binding bracelets that allow her to control the wyverns when she puts one on them."

Amber took several steps back from him before she did a slow turn, frowning as she tried to figure out exactly where her and Ronan had entered the world. A pity he hadn't given her the time to grab her caged Pliethin. Then she would have had a thread she would have been able to use to travel through the Void.

"We're wasting time," Tathen growled. "For all we know, she's in league with Brigitte. It wouldn't be the first time Brigitte's staged something to allow someone to infiltrate our people. I won't allow Brigitte to take any more of my family from me."

"Give her a chance," the first dragon said.

Tathen faced the dragon. "It's not like you have anyone to lose at the camp, Becan."

"We all mourned the loss of your wife and sons," Becan said. "They were our family too."

Worried a fight might start, Amber was relieved to finally figure out the direction. "That way." She remained facing the direction of where she'd arrived. "About twenty minutes' flight."

The dragons shapeshifted. Becan collected Jorn while Tathen, who'd shot into the sky, returned and allowed Cort to scramble onto his back before taking to the air again. Morgane formed her dragon wings. "If you truly aren't one of Brigitte's people then come with us and protect our people from those sent to attack us. Unless the sword at your side and the daggers at your wrists are for decoration."

Amber didn't hesitate. She had no idea who was in the wrong in their war, but she knew that Brigitte wasn't her friend. Not while she held Ronan against his will. "Lead the way." She changed into a goshawk, taking to the sky.

Morgane led the way, flying at a faster pace than earlier. They heard the sounds of battle before they reached the clearing. Ahead, Amber saw the two dragons and the hunters join the battle. Approximately thirty people fought the hybrids and their hunters. They were the ones that Amber had noticed when Ronan had brought her out of the Void. It didn't take her long to realise that even outnumbered, the hybrids fought with a ferocity and recklessness that Morgane's people couldn't match. She doubted there'd be anyone who could, other than an actual wyvern.

Amber landed at the edge of the clearing near a still body. Blood stained the chest, but she could hear a heartbeat. Jorn and Becan kept a hybrid from the young man. Amber crouched at his side, pressing her hands against the wound, relieved when she discovered he was half dragon. She couldn't heal humans unless they had enough dragon blood in them. She glanced at the bracelets on her arms above her wrist sheaths. There might not be enough power to draw on with the amount of fighting that was going on around her.

The young man tried to sit up when his wound closed, his white blond hair plastered to his head from blood. "You have my thanks, whoever you are."

Amber tried to push him back down. "You've lost a lot of blood."

He grinned. "Then I guess I'll have to take theirs to replace it." As soon as he was standing, he became a dragon and launched himself into the air to fight one of the hybrid wyverns that hadn't shifted into human form.

Slowly shaking her head, Amber glanced around the area. She spotted a young man healing the injured, the task far too big for one person. She hurried towards him, hoping he'd be able to point out which ones had dragon ancestry. She wasn't sure if there were enough to fight the hybrids, but if someone didn't heal the wounded, they wouldn't live long enough to have a chance to win.

The healer reached for a dagger when he noticed Amber's approach.

She held up her bloodstained hands. "Morgane brought me with her to help. I can only heal those with dragon ancestry. As long as it's not too diluted."

The healer gestured to the woman he was trying to save. "Half dragon."

Amber knelt beside the woman, pressing her hands against the gashes criss-crossing her body. "I've got this." She focused on healing the woman, trying to ignore how the healer watched her. She didn't blame him. He didn't know her. She was halfway through healing the woman when he moved onto the next injured person.

It wasn't until they were each healing their fourth patient that he looked over to Amber. "I'm Rainer."

She smiled wearily at him, needing to draw power from one of her bracelets. "Amber."

"Where do you come from? Your ability to heal far exceeds ours."

She had no idea how to answer him. Brisbane? The name of the town she sometimes lived in would mean nothing to him. Nor would telling him Australia. Although these days she spent more time at Temolae Keep in the dragons' world than anywhere else. "These days I'm mostly living in the world Brigitte came from. Before that, I lived in a different world."

He looked up from the girl he healed. "You travel between the worlds?"

She started to protest then realised, that in a way, it was true. "This is the fourth world I've travel to."

"That surprises you?" He moved onto another patient.

Chapter Four

Before Amber had a chance to answer, a hybrid, in human form, barrelled past the warrior he fought and threw himself at Rainer. Amber automatically shifted into her panther form, leaping on the hybrid before he could plunge his swords into Rainer.

The hybrid snarled, echoing the sound Amber made. He struggled to break free from her, having lost one of his swords when she'd knocked him to the ground.

She kept him pinned down, the ferocity of his movements reminding her of the way wyverns attacked. As soon as she had the chance, she went for his throat, sinking her teeth in, the warm blood filling her mouth. Even as he died, he continued to fight, his movements growing weaker until he stilled. The beating of his heart stopped. Drawing away from him, she shifted into human form, scanning the area to see that no hybrids were coming for them. She wiped her mouth on her shirt, trying not to think of the blood that the panther in her had savoured. As long as she didn't think about it, she'd be okay and wouldn't be throwing up in front of possible allies.

Rainer stared at Amber, dagger in hand as he stood by one of his patients.

Amber glanced at the warrior who'd returned to the fight before she crouched at the side of the dragon she'd been trying to heal. She nodded to Rainer's patient. "I can't help you with that one. They're human."

He sheathed his dagger, looking between Amber and the patient as he crouched at their side. "What are you? I thought you were a healer."

She grinned. "I am. But I'm more than that." She felt her grin take on the feel of Ronan's predatory smile. "Much more." She almost apologised when she saw the startled look in Rainer's eyes. She remained silent. No one knew her and Ronan here. She wasn't about to die in some unknown world and would use whatever it took to get the two of them back to their worlds. And to the people who waited for them.

Rainer sent frequent looks towards Amber as the two of them continued to work on their patients, sometimes warriors dropping wounded off for them and sometimes the wounded staggering over to where they worked. The two of them were kept busy healing the injured, the sounds of fighting all around them.

The sun was no longer overhead by the time Amber realised the sounds of fighting had lessened. She struggled to rise, exhaustion washing over her as a warrior she'd just healed stumbled towards the fighting. She almost called out after him to demand what had been the point in healing him. But it wasn't like he could do anything else. Seeing there were no dragons for her to heal, she turned to Rainer. "I'll help the warriors." Before he had a chance to reply, she shapeshifted and took to the air, flying towards the closest hybrid who was in wyvern form and airborne. There were three of them. Only two left on the ground. She landed on his back, becoming human.

The hybrid roared, spiralling through the sky as he aimed for the ground.

Amber clung with her knees, plunging her daggers into his back to help her keep her seat. Every time they were upright, she let go of one of the daggers long enough to launch a fireball at a wing. Before he crashed into the ground, she withdrew her daggers, sheathed them and leapt from his back. She shifted into a goshawk and flew away from him, crying out in triumph as he crashed into the ground.

The hybrid shapeshifted to human form and struggled to rise to his feet as he drew a sword.

Amber landed in front of him at the same time as one of Morgane's people came up behind him. Turning human, she launched fireballs at him, trying not to think of how exhausted she was and how many bracelets she'd drawn power from. Ronan would have called her an idiot with how much power she'd used. But he wasn't here to help her. And she wasn't about to ally herself with someone who had kids so they could eat their hearts. About to launch another fireball, she stopped when the hybrid collapsed between her and the young man she'd saved when she'd arrived at the camp.

He grinned at her. "Nice moves. Where've you been hiding?"

A glance around showed that all the wyverns and hunters were dead or captured. She lowered her hands, closing the one that still held a fireball, extinguishing it. "Not in this world."

Morgane landed beside the young man. "What are you doing here, Treon? You're not Gold. Brigitte will have no interest in you. There was no need for you to risk yourself like this." Morgane looked him up and down. "Don't you think Rainer has enough work without you adding to it?"

He enveloped Morgane in his arms. "I missed you too, Mum."

Morgane sighed, returning his hug before holding him from her. "None of you listen and always have to go your own way."

He grinned. "Wonder where we get that from."

Amber stared at him. "You're Ronan's grandson?" It was hard to think of him as having grandchildren. For all she knew, he might have a tonne of them. He probably made an even worse grandfather than he did a father. Not that she was an expert when it came to grandfathers. Look at hers. Most of the time he wanted to kill her. And that wasn't a figure of speech.

Treon shrugged. "Who is Ronan?"

"Forget about Ronan for now," Morgane said. "You need to see Rainer."

Amber scanned his body. None of the wounds she'd healed had reopened. They were new ones. "I can help."

Morgane stepped between Amber and Treon. "Rainer will heal him."

"It's not like I haven't already-"

Treon interrupted Amber, briefly pressing a finger to his lips in a hushing motion. "She was helping

Rainer while we fought. I trust her." He stepped around Morgane, smiling down at Amber. "Maybe you could tell me about the world you're from while you heal me."

Before Amber could say anything, Jorn joined them. "Starne said he saw one of the hybrids flying towards the castle partway through the attack. We need to leave before they return with more warriors."

Amber placed her hands on Treon's wounds, healing him, glad Jorn's arrival meant she didn't need to talk about herself. "Are you going to retaliate?" There was no way she'd be able to attack the castle on her own. And without Ronan, she had no way of returning home. Returning to Kade, Crystal and Rian. And all the other people she'd give her life to protect.

Treon smiled at Amber as she finished healing him. "Thanks." His smile faded. "We should have attacked her back when we had more warriors. Not have left her to grow strong."

"We need to focus on what to do now." Jorn slipped his arm around Morgane's waist. "We'll find somewhere else to hide, then make plans."

Around Amber, people packed up the few canvas tents that hadn't been destroyed and put out the campfire. "Where are you going?" She wasn't about to be left behind.

"Closer to Brigitte's castle," Morgane said.

Treon faced Morgane. "We're going after her?"

Morgane didn't answer immediately. "I won't have her kill one of you." She rested her hand on Treon's arm. "None of you." She glanced around the clearing before facing Amber. "If you stay with us, you will be watched. I'm not about to fall for another one of her tricks."

Tathen joined them. "How did Brigitte know where to find us?"

Amber mentally searched the area. No one was hidden nearby. The only ones she could find were those in the clearing packing up.

"We need to figure that out." Morgane stepped away from her family. "Later. Right now, we need to leave. It won't take her long to send more hybrids after us. And we can't face another battle right now. We need time to recover."

Amber helped them pack. Not that they had much. A few personal items, some clothes, canvas tents, cookware, basic crockery and utensils. It was hard to believe some of them were dragons considering how little they had. All the dragons she knew loved to hoard, especially land and wealth.

As they left the area, she noticed a hybrid in wyvern form, along with a rider, come in close. Both were hidden. They remained close as they headed in the direction of the castle, all of them either flying or riding a dragon. Amber flew towards the hybrid and rider, mentally reaching for Morgane. She had no idea what the hybrid and rider planned to do, but doubted it'd be good. *"There's a hybrid to my right. Following alongside us."*

Morgane flew close to Amber, once again in a winged human form. *"Attack the hunter. That's who's hiding them. We can attack them once you break the hunter's concentration."*

Amber hoped Morgane was right. She flew at the rider's face. He threw up his hands to protect his face, struggling to stay on the wyvern. The moment he was visible, Morgane, Jorn, Becan, Tathen, Cort and Treon attacked the two of them. Amber helped, aiming for the wyvern's wings. She flew out of the way of the claws, the hunter plummeting past her towards the ground.

Treon, in dragon form, grabbed hold of him before he hit the ground.

"We need to get out of here before more arrive," Morgane said aloud.

Amber sensed a group of hybrids in wyvern form

ridden by hunters. *"It's too late. Twenty hybrids and their riders coming in fast."*

"Treon, protect everyone. We'll meet at the usual place. All of you hide. Jorn, Becan, Cort, Tathen and I will hold them off to give you a chance to get away," Morgane said.

Amber flew out ahead of the group, going for the face of the hunter in the lead. He and the hybrid became visible. *"I'll attack the hunters. You keep them from going invisible again."*

"We won't be able to hold them for long," Jorn warned.

Amber dodged an attack, the hybrids and hunters focusing on her. Nearby she sensed a Pliethin. If only she knew how to make caged Pliethins. But the Knight Mages hadn't been willing to share the details. *"Can any of your dragons use a Pliethin yet?"*

"There are very few Golds in this world and none of us know how to use one." Morgane flew above one of the visible hunters and hybrids, swooping down on them. *"Brigitte told me very little about them when I was younger."*

"There's one nearby." Amber flew at the face of a hidden hunter, nearly caught by a hybrid who came to his defence. She plummeted towards the ground, pulling up at the last second, the hybrid following her.

One of the hybrids raked his claws across Jorn's arm. *"We can't hold them off much longer."*

"Time to separate and escape." Morgane flew in the direction of the castle, the others going in different directions.

Amber wasn't sure who to follow. She strengthened her ties to Morgane and Jorn so she'd be able to find them if they were separated. The two of them seemed to be the leaders. She flew towards the ground again, skimming the tops of the trees, diving beneath the canopy when a hybrid continued to follow her. Sensing Morgane and Jorn head away from her, she tried to lose the hybrid and hunter following her. She certainly had a lot to say to Ronan when she saw him again. Particularly about not giving her the chance to grab a caged Pliethin. He better not let himself be killed. She didn't want to be stuck in this world. There were too many people waiting for her.

Seeing a hollow log ahead, she dived inside it, landing and staying still. The hybrid continued to fly overhead, another one behind him. She remained where she was, staying in her goshawk form. Around her she heard the sounds of the forest creatures, some of their smells enticing. Having breakfast was yet one more thing Ronan hadn't given her time to do before they left. She was starving. Peeking outside the hollow log, she scanned the area. It seemed safe enough. Once outside the log, she shapeshifted into a panther. It looked like she'd need to hunt down her own food. She hated not being able to cook it. At least in one of her animal forms she didn't mind raw food. In those forms she actually preferred it.

Before she went hunting, she checked where Morgane and Jorn were. They'd changed directions. From this distance she couldn't tell if they were being followed. She'd hunt them down once she'd eaten. It wasn't good to let herself get too hungry. That was when the wild animals inside her wanted to take over and she needed to be clear headed. She wanted to go home.

It didn't take her long to catch a rabbit and eat it, all the while trying to focus on other things. Like what she'd say to Ronan. He couldn't keep expecting to come up with lame excuses when he wanted her to do something for him. If he'd really believed she'd owed him for saving her life, he would have said something sooner. Maybe. Although who knew when it came to Ronan. But she would have words with him.

Chapter Five

Finished eating, Amber leapt into the air, shapeshifting into a goshawk and taking to the sky. There were no hybrids nearby. There were also none of Morgane's people. She should have strengthened her sense of Treon. The more people she could keep track of in this precarious world, the better her chances were of surviving. He'd been sent to safety. She needed to think like Ronan. Not that she knew what he would have done other than look after himself in the same sort of situation. He better be okay.

Spotting Morgane in the distance, Amber sensed two hybrids trailing her, both with hunters riding on them and all four of them invisible. Did Morgane know she was being followed? Picking up speed, Amber attacked one of the hunters. Those two focused on her, the other two continuing to follow

Morgane. *"You've got a hybrid and hunter following you."*

"That is a useful ability."

"I'll keep these two busy and when I lose them, I'll come and help you with the ones still following you." Amber flew towards the forest, the air colder here compared to where Morgane's people had been camped.

"How did you find me?" Morgane headed in the direction of the castle again.

Amber wasn't sure how much to tell her. How many times had Ronan told her that knowledge was power? *"It's one of my abilities."*

"Can you find anyone?"

She flew below the canopy, dodging between trees as the hybrid and hunter tried to follow her.

"Amber?"

"I can barely hear you. The distance between us is getting too great." At least now she had time to think about what to say. Unless Morgane forgot about their conversation. She had a feeling that wasn't likely to happen.

It didn't take long for her to lose the hybrid and hunter, the hybrid having shapeshifted to search around the bushes she'd flown into. She slipped out the other side when the two of them looked in the wrong spot for her. Seeking out Morgane, she flew in her direction, hoping the distance between Brigitte's people was too great for them to communicate with each other.

It was well after dark by the time Amber had helped Morgane and her people evade the hybrids and hunters following them. Morgane led the way to a cave where a fire was set out the front, deer cooking over it. Morgane landed in front of Treon, who rose from the rock he was sitting on.

Amber landed near Morgane, trying to ignore the weariness that tugged at her. She wanted to crawl into bed and sleep for a week. After the amount of interrupted nights and today's fights, she struggled to stay upright.

Morgane smiled as her gaze travelled across those seated around the fire or in front of one of the canvas tents that had been erected. "You all escaped."

Jorn joined them, clapping his son on the shoulder. "There's nothing wrong at the village? Ninian is well? And Cort and Anja's daughter?"

Treon nodded. "Ninian and Runa are well. As is Edvin. He wanted to join me." Treon grinned. "He's been talking about exploring the world like his grandfather." He glanced at Cort before returning his attention to his parents. "The hunter we captured tried to escape. He didn't survive the attempt."

Morgane inclined her head. "No one else was hurt?"

When Treon shook his head, Amber wanted to demand what they planned to do. She didn't know any of the people they talked about. Instead of interrupting, she remained silent. The fact that they wanted to know about friends and family was reassuring. There were obviously people they cared about.

Morgane turned to Becan, giving him a nod before leaving Treon by the fire, Jorn following her.

Amber watched them walk away, wishing she could find out what they were planning. She didn't even know if she should follow them. It wasn't like they'd even looked in her direction. She took a step towards them, the distance between them growing greater. Her body protested the effort.

Treon beckoned Amber over, taking two plates of food from a man sitting by the fire. He smiled when she remained where she was, glancing between him and his parents.

The food won out and she forced her legs to move, taking the plate he handed her. "Thanks."

"You were going to tell me about your world." He led the way to a log that was several metres away from the fire.

Amber sat beside him, somehow managing not to collapse on it in an undignified heap. It was close though. "My life isn't that interesting."

"Do you have someone waiting for you back in your world?" Treon asked.

She nodded, eating some food.

"Someone with your abilities?"

"No. A dragon." She couldn't help wondering what Kade was doing. Was he worried about how long she'd been gone? Or did he think she was okay because she was with Ronan and he had no choice other than to protect her?

Treon chuckled. "I should have known with how skilled you are as a warrior."

Amber didn't bother telling him she hadn't always been so skilled. She stifled a yawn. "Who are the people you were talking about before? Ninian, Runa and Edvin." She needed to know more about them. Who they were and if they could be trusted.

"Ninian is one of my younger sisters. The oldest one out of the two of them. We've been staying with Runa and her son Edvin. Runa is Cort and Anja's daughter."

Amber couldn't help wondering exactly how many grandchildren Ronan had in this world. "You have two sisters?" Again she struggled to stifle a yawn. As much as she needed sleep, she needed information more.

Treon shook his head. "Three sisters. Tanith is the oldest and is Gold. She was married with young children of her own when Brigitte first came after us." His gaze collided with a fair-haired woman sitting with a group of people who were talking and laughing, some of them boasting about their exploits earlier that day. She smiled at him, nodding before she turned to the person beside her. Treon returned his attention to Amber. "Some of my parents' people went with Tanith to one of the countries Cort discovered during his travels with Tathen. It's not safe here for a gold. We haven't seen her and her family for centuries. It's safer for them."

Amber glanced several times at the fair-haired woman, wondering what she'd told Treon. "And your younger sister?"

He nodded towards the fair-haired woman. "Keeley. She's Gold like Tanith, but she was a hatchling when Tanith and her family left. Too young to go with them."

Now she wanted to know even more what their exchange had been about. "I'm sorry you haven't seen some of your family for so long." Amber was tempted to ask him how old he was, but didn't think it would be polite.

Treon shrugged. "They're with people who'll keep them safe. Devona went with them. Along with Hella and her brothers. Devona is cunning and Hella's fierce. Between the two of them, my sister and her family will be safe. A lot safer than those of us here."

She had so many questions she wanted to ask him, but guessed it wasn't the best idea to fire them at him one at a time like she was interrogating him. It also didn't help that she was so tired it was an effort to function. "Do you think your parents will allow Ronan to take Brigitte back to her own world?"

Treon shrugged. "It's possible. I know Mum doesn't want to be the one to kill Brigitte, but she also doesn't think it's right for her to expect someone else to do the job she can't do." Treon paused a moment. "What is my grandfather like?"

This time it was Amber who shrugged. She had no idea how to describe Ronan. "He's different from most people I know. Including dragons." She slowly shook her head, wishing she could describe him a little better. She still couldn't get her head around Ronan having grandchildren. He didn't look old enough. But she supposed dragons didn't age like humans.

Treon looked towards his parents, giving a single nod before turning to Amber. "How does this sensing those that are hidden by hunter magic work for you?"

It would be nice if he could ask her questions that she could actually answer. "I can feel them there. Like being able to see them with my mind."

"You can sense their signature?" Treon asked.

"I guess. Maybe. I'm not exactly sure what you mean by their signature so I can only guess." Considering they spoke her language, which until this moment she hadn't even stopped to think they might have spoken another language, she couldn't always understand them. "How is it you speak the same language I do?"

"There have been other travellers over the centuries. Ones stranded here that have come through when connections between other worlds become available. But those connections didn't last and they were stranded here. Mum has always been interested in seeing how the languages changed over the centuries in the worlds her family came from."

Amber wondered if those times had been when the bindings were weak or were being redone. She doubted anyone could tell her for certain. "So you chose to speak their language?"

Treon grinned. "I've learned many languages in

my life. This is one that seems more common to those who come through to our world." He glanced at Morgane. "How far can you be from someone and still detect their signature?"

She nearly said that Morgane could ask her own questions if she wanted to know the answers. She pushed aside her feelings of irritation knowing they were because of how tired she was. "Depends on how well I know them." She glanced in the direction of Morgane and Jorn, aware of where they were every time they moved. Remembering how Treon had been the one to take everyone to safety, she focused on learning his signature, as he called it. For good measure, she also learned the signature of his sister, Keeley. Like the dragons' world, Golds were important here. Even if it was for a different reason.

"Would you join us in scouting Brigitte's castle? Hunters can't use their magic to remain hidden within the castle, even Brigitte's warriors, but that still leaves them a lot of places where they can hide and see us if we try to enter the castle."

Amber grinned at him. "I've been asking Morgane about returning to the castle ever since we left it."

"I'll assume that is a yes."

She laughed. "It is yes." Her laughter faded along with the small burst of energy that had filled her at the thought of finally being able to rescue Ronan and get out of this place. "When do we leave? What is the rest of the plan?"

"That will depend on what we find." He held her gaze. "You still interested in helping?"

"I'm not about to leave Ronan with Brigitte." Even if he wasn't her only way out of here, she still wouldn't have left him with Brigitte. He'd kept his promise to Brigitte and look how she'd repaid him. Ronan didn't deserve that. No one did. "When do we go?"

"Daylight. I'll have someone find you warmer dragon-leather clothes. It gets rather cold at Brigitte's castle."

Amber again stifled a yawn, wishing she could curl up somewhere and sleep even though it was nowhere near bedtime. At this point the ground was starting to look comfortable. "You don't need to tell me how cold it is." At movement to her left, she looked in that direction, tensing in preparation to form a fireball and throw it. "Rainer." She tried to relax, but she remained tense and alert, tiredness temporarily fading at the rush of adrenaline.

Rainer nodded towards her plate that was now empty. "Did you want anything else to eat?"

"I'm right." She handed over the plate when he held out his hand.

"Could we ask you to look at a few minor wounds?"

She wanted to ask him to let her sleep instead. She turned to Treon. "Are we done?" She was half tempted to beg him to say no. The thought of moving to do anything other than stumble somewhere out of the way to sleep was daunting.

Treon nodded.

Trying not to sigh, Amber slowly rose to her feet and followed Rainer. She was kept busy until it drew close to bedtime when Keeley collected her and took her to a river where she could wash. The evening was cool so Amber hurriedly washed, glad to crawl between the blankets she was shown to in one of the tents. She shared the tent with Keeley and another dragon she was introduced to. Morgane's younger sister, Caral, who was also Gold. Before going to sleep, Amber strengthened her ties to Caral. No matter what happened, she would have at least one person in this world. Without allies she wouldn't survive.

Tempted to create a link with everyone in the camp, she told herself not to be stupid. She needed sleep and shouldn't be staying up all night making ties to people who'd never be important to her. She couldn't help thinking about Kade. What was he doing right now? And Crystal and Rian. Were they worried? Trying to find her? Forcing herself to close her eyes, she tried to focus on sleeping. As tired as she was, the many thoughts and fears kept her from dropping off to sleep as quickly as she'd expected to. She must have fallen asleep at some stage, because Morgane woke her before daylight with a light brush across her mind.

Chapter Six

Amber joined the small group at the fire, once she was dressed in thick dragon-leather trousers and a long sleeve shirt, taking the plate of food Treon handed her. No one spoke while they ate, most of the camp around them silent. Only the soft sounds of people sleeping and a couple of people patrolling the area disturbed the quiet of the slowly lightening morning. Amber would have preferred it if someone had talked so she could focus on anything other than her thoughts. She couldn't stop worrying about how everyone was back home. The couple of trackers they had weren't very skilled. Surely Kade wouldn't risk letting one of them lead him through the Void to find her.

Morgane, Jorn, Cort and Becan seemed to rise as one while Tathen, Starne and Treon stood up a few seconds after them. When Becan, Tathen, Starne and

Treon shifted into their dragon form, Jorn clambered onto Starne's back and Cort onto Tathen's.

Morgane made her way to Amber, nodding towards her son. "I noticed yesterday that you rode your dragon to the castle. Treon offered to carry you."

"Thanks."

"No, thank you." Morgane met Amber's gaze a moment longer before she clambered onto Becan's back, the two of them taking to the sky followed by the other four.

As soon as Amber was seated, Treon took off after them. She clung to him, her legs tightening around him in an effort to stay seated. "Do you ever use saddles?"

"We lost a lot of our things when Brigitte sent a few hundred hybrids against our castle. We were lucky so many of us escaped with our lives. If you'd visited us a year ago, you would have had a much more comfortable stay with us."

Amber had no idea what to say to him. And she'd thought her grandmother sucked. Obviously she wasn't anywhere near as bad as a dragon grandmother. The air grew cold against her hands and face, but the rest of her stayed warm. Scanning the area, she found no one. None that were visible and none that were hidden. She didn't know if that was good or bad. "Aren't there many people in your world?"

"Not in this area. It's too close to where the savages live. They attack anyone who comes near their lands. It's easiest to stay away from them. Although if they try to invade our territory again, we might raid theirs."

Amber grinned. That second comment was the sort of thing she expected to hear from a dragon, not the first one. Her grin faded. She needed to find a way home to her dragons. Longing for Kade washed over her and she pushed it away. She had to focus on what needed to be done, not pine away for Kade and home. Not that the fierce feeling she'd felt seemed at all like pining.

In the distance she saw the snow-capped mountain, the castle rapidly coming into view. It wouldn't be long and they'd be close enough for her to search the area. The air grew colder and she wished they'd given her gloves. Much further and they would be in clear view of the patrolling warriors. "I can sense hybrids around the castle." She jumped from Treon's back, shifting into a goshawk. *I'll let you know what I find. Let your family know not to go any closer or they'll be spotted.*

"You can't go in there alone," Treon protested.

"It's okay, people don't notice birds. I can sneak in and find out how many warriors Brigitte has." Amber flew towards the Castle, continually scanning the area for enemies. She noticed that Morgane's people stayed well back. Treon must have passed along the message.

"I can bend the light around us to hide us from view. Why risk them noticing you approaching when it isn't necessary," Treon offered. *"I can hide our sounds and scents from them too."*

Amber slowed, allowing him to come alongside her. Glancing to the side, she saw nothing. *"You're a dragon."* Had the dragons somehow evolved differently in this world?

Humour was clear in his thoughts. *"My father is a hunter. Ninian and I have the abilities of hunters. We think it might be to do with the fact we aren't Gold. I'm directly below you. Land on my back and I'll be able to hide you from view too."*

She hadn't needed him to tell her where he was. She'd sensed him change location. Dropping down the short distance, she was surprised when the light appeared to bend around her. *"Why are you sharing all this information with me? Aren't you worried what I might do with it?"*

Once again there was humour in his thoughts. *"Should I be?"*

She stared at the castle as they continued to come closer to it. They headed towards an open window on one of the upper floors. *"You might want to go to the window to the left, the one you're flying towards has a hybrid and hunter in front of it."* She paused a moment as he altered the direction he flew in. *"I have no plans to do anything with the information, but you don't know that. You don't know me."*

He stopped in front of the window. *"I do know you. I saw your expression as you tried to save my people. My family. You would have been devastated if you'd lost any of them. Tell me I'm wrong."*

The moment Amber left his back so she could enter the castle window, she became visible. *"I might not use any information against you, but I can't promise the same goes for my ally. I can't keep news from Ronan that would be of use to him."* Checking both directions, mentally and visually, she flew to the doorway of the bedroom. Luckily it was open and she was able to remain in goshawk form.

"Does he offer you the same courtesy?"

She was tempted to laugh, but didn't dare risk making any noise. She had no idea how well sounds travelled in this castle. *"Everyone has a tendency to ask that question."* Landing on the floor, she peered out into an empty hallway. The way was clear. She searched for Ronan, sensing him below and off to her left.

"I notice you didn't confirm that he does," Treon said.

Sensing someone coming towards her, Amber slipped into the nearby room, having checked first that there was no one inside. *"Ronan has his own way of doing things."* She landed on the floor in the room, remaining close to the door.

"So in other words, he doesn't." When Amber didn't answer him, Treon spoke again. *"How long will it take you to discover how many warriors Brigitte has?"*

She'd known the moment she'd entered the castle, but she wasn't about to share the news with him. She wanted to talk to Ronan before she left. *"Sorry, I can't talk. I need to concentrate on where everyone is so I don't run into any of them."*

"I hope you're not planning to rescue Ronan. It's too dangerous to do that on your own."

"I am not an idiot." She was glad he didn't know her well enough to argue that comment. She might have done a few crazy things, but nothing she hadn't thought she'd had a chance of surviving. Mostly.

"I'd feel better if you actually said you had no plans to rescue him right this moment." He paused. *"My parents are asking how much longer this will take."*

Sensing the person in the hallway was coming closer, Amber flew under the bed. *"Are they okay?"* She mentally searched for each of them. They seemed to be well back from the hidden warriors. *"Can they stay hidden much longer?"*

"That isn't what concerns them. They're worried about those who've stayed behind. As am I."

"I'll be as–" Amber broke off when someone entered the room. *"Quiet for a minute. I have someone right next to me."* She backed away from the edge of the bed as a woman drew near. Her steps were brisk and she leaned over the bed, shifting the linen before striding from the room. Amber tried to think if the bed had been made when she'd entered. She was pretty certain it had been. So what had the woman been doing? She crept forward, peeking out from under the bed. Once again the room was clear. She flew up to check the bed. The sheets had been turned down.

Landing on the floor, she cautiously made her way forward, one step at a time as she mentally searched the area. The woman who'd entered the room was well away from her, on a lower floor of the castle.

Ronan was still in the same place and most of the warriors scattered about the castle hadn't moved, the majority of them outside. Brigitte had to have several hundred people. She had no idea how she was going to get Ronan out of here. Not with the amount of people they had to get past.

"*Are you all right?*" Treon asked. "*What do I tell my family?*"

"*The majority of Brigitte's warriors are outside, hidden. There aren't anywhere near as many inside.*" She stepped into the hallway, looking in both directions even though she couldn't sense anybody nearby.

"*How many do they have? We need specific numbers.*"

"*It's hard to count when they keep moving around.*" Amber headed along the hallway. "*At least several hundred people. Maybe as many as five hundred.*"

"*You need to get out immediately. It isn't safe in there. You can't imagine what it's like to face a horde of her hybrids. The amount we faced yesterday is nothing in comparison. This won't be all she has. There will be hybrids in her villages that are scattered around the mountain.*"

Amber couldn't keep the amusement from the tone of her words. "*I didn't expect to be safe.*" She could have told him that the situations Ronan got her in were rarely safe.

"What are you doing in there? Do you need me to create a distraction so you can escape?"

Amber tilted her head on the side. Ronan was being moved? She took a step forward. Yes, he was definitely being moved. What did Brigitte plan? Was she going to kill him? Pain arrowed through her at the thought of being stuck here. Of never being able to see Kade again. Of losing Ronan. She wasn't about to let any of that happen.

"Amber? Are you still there?"

She started to reply to Treon, stopping when she realised Ronan was walking beside the woman who'd turned down the bed sheets. They were headed in her direction.

"Amber. Can you answer me?"

The worry in his voice caught her attention. *"Sorry. I won't be much longer."* Flying low, she skimmed across the floor of the hallway and headed back into the bedroom to hide under the bed.

"What are you doing?"

She looked first in the direction of the doorway then towards the window that she could see from where she stood under the bed. A clanging of chains proceeded Ronan and the woman. Amber was tempted to peek out from underneath the bed to see what was happening, but she remained where she was, contacting Treon instead. *"If I move, I'll be spotted."*

"I can cause a distraction," Treon reminded her.

"That isn't necessary," Amber said. *"They'll move on and then I can leave."* Hopefully once she'd spoken to Ronan.

The woman stopped by the bed. "Brigitte won't be long." She strode from the room, leaving Ronan behind, her footsteps brisk.

Amber peeked out from under the bed, mentally searching the area as well. Finding it clear, she stepped out and shapeshifted. A grin formed when she saw Ronan was chained to the wall near the bed head. "Enjoying your reunion?" Her gaze momentarily rested on the chains.

"I hope you're not here to tell me you're about to rescue me, kitten," Ronan said.

"Not today. So why don't you want to be rescued?"

"I never said I didn't want to be rescued. Only that I hope you're not about to rescue me."

Amber barely managed not to sigh. "Don't be difficult, Ronan." She automatically kept scanning the area, making sure no one was headed towards the bedroom. "What is going on?"

"It seems that Brigitte is in need of a Gold heart and the two of us had not one, but two Golds in the past."

For a few seconds she couldn't speak. "You're not going to let her eat the heart of a child. And not only a child, but her own kid."

Ronan's predatory smile formed and he closed the distance between them. "Do you really think I'd waste an offspring of mine like that if they were Gold?"

"No. So why are you thinking of having a kid with her?"

"A deal has already been struck."

"What is the deal? Will it interfere with the promise you made her? Or is that no longer an issue?" She ignored Treon when he called out to her, needing to focus on the conversation and scanning the area.

"Give me a week."

She wanted to protest, but it was too late. "Brigitte is on her way here." She took a step towards the window. "How do you know Brigitte will keep her end of the bargain?"

"She isn't about to try and kill me until after the egg hatches." Ronan's predatory smile formed again. "Unlike you, she can't tell what it will be until it's born."

Chapter Seven

Amber took another step towards the window, glancing at the doorway before she returned her attention to Ronan. "Don't get yourself killed." She pointed a finger at him. "You better not get me stuck here." Turning into a goshawk, she flew outside, mentally reaching for Treon who flew towards her.

"There's someone watching you at the window," Treon warned.

Amber didn't need to look. *"It's Ronan."*

"That's my grandfather?"

"Yeah." She landed on his back and he hid her like he continued to hide himself.

"What do those from his country think of him?" Treon flew towards his family.

Finding it difficult to remain on his back in her goshawk form, Amber shapeshifted, leaning forward to hold on to him, speaking aloud now it was possible. "That he's not someone to mess with."

"That might help him when dealing with Brigitte, but I doubt it," Treon said.

Amber didn't know what to say. Obviously it had helped. He'd negotiated a deal that would keep him alive for now. Ronan might not appreciate her telling anyone about his plans, but knowing they didn't have to rush in and save him might be important. "She's not interested in killing him. He's Gold and the two of them have had Gold offspring before."

"Someone who'll be able to provide her with Gold hearts. We should have known she'd choose that course." Treon changed direction slightly.

Amber noticed that his family did the same, keeping ahead of him. "That doesn't make sense. Ronan offered to take her back to her world where she'd have access to an endless supply of Gold hearts. Why would she stay here instead?"

Treon landed in a clearing where his family awaited him, shifting once Amber was off his back. He studied her, frowning. "There must be a reason. She wouldn't stay here when she can return to her world. From what I've been told, it's something she's always wanted."

Morgane looked from one to the other. "What is going on?"

Treon explained their conversation.

Morgane slowly nodded. "We need to find out what she's really planning. She's been wanting to return home for centuries. Unless she's learned something about her home to make her change her mind. We can't rely on her leaving our world in peace. We will have to see to it ourselves that she's no longer a threat." Morgane briefly smiled up at Jorn when he slid an arm around her waist, drawing her close. She held his gaze a moment before nodding and turning to Amber. "Where are all of Brigitte's warriors stationed?"

Using leaves and twigs to represent the castle and wall, Amber pointed out the locations of the sentries and the path of the handful that had been patrolling. She rose to her feet, meeting Morgane's gaze. "You'd need an army to take the place."

"We don't need an army, only someone who can take Brigitte out," Morgane stated.

Jorn still had his arm around Morgane's waist. "You're not an assassin and I can't imagine you letting anyone else do something you're unwilling to do."

Morgane sighed. "We can't continue to let her do

this. She'll never change. And now we have two of them to deal with."

"Ronan won't allow her to kill a child of his." He was too possessive, but she didn't know if telling them that would make things better or worse. "I don't know what his plans are, but he'll have his own reasons for wanting a Gold child. And they won't involve killing it for its heart."

"How can you be certain he won't want the child's heart?" Becan asked.

"The eating of hearts has been outlawed," Amber said. "Only renegades still eat them."

"That would give her a reason to stay here," Jorn said. "Would Ronan have told her?"

Amber shrugged.

"She's not going to want to go home if things have changed that much," Morgane said. "There is no way she'll willingly return home."

Amber grinned. "Who's to say it has to be willing?"

"No one can force Brigitte to do anything against her will," Morgane stated.

"If she's never held a Pliethin, then there's no way she'll be able to stop Ronan from taking her through the Void to her home." Amber smiled, remembering trying to prevent Ronan from taking her into the Void. "Or unless she has access to a caged Pliethin."

"None of us know how to use them," Morgane said. "Not that there are many Golds in our world. Most of us tend to live very short lives."

"Can you sneak into the castle again and ask Ronan what Brigitte's plans might be?" Becan asked.

Treon took a step forward, shaking his head. "We can't ask that of her. It's too dangerous."

Jorn smiled. "I have a feeling she's seen more than her share of danger." He paused a moment, studying Amber. "We wouldn't expect you to go in there without help, but you're the only one who is capable of sensing where hunters are when we bend the light around ourselves."

Amber nodded. Returning to the castle suited her perfectly. She needed to find out what Ronan was planning so they could get out of here. Before something happened to him and she was stuck in this world forever. "I can do it." Not many Dragon Mages could sense people when they were hiding so she was lucky she'd ended up with that ability.

Morgane looked at each of her companions. "Then it's settled? We return to camp and find somewhere safer for everyone then help Amber make contact with Ronan so we can learn what Brigitte knows and what her plans might be."

"What if he doesn't know her plans?" Jorn asked.

"We need to kill her before she can kill any more of us," Tathen said. "We've all lost too many. We can't afford to lose any more."

"I'll see that she's stopped," Morgane stated.

Becan stepped closer to Morgane. "It isn't your burden alone. We all thought she wouldn't survive the mountains let alone thrive in them."

"I should have known," Morgane said. "She has always been willing to do whatever it takes to survive. Things no one else would consider doing."

Morgane's words made her think of Ronan. Hadn't he done similar? For a second she wondered at her own sanity for having entwined her life with his. Drawing in a deep breath, she pushed aside her concerns. There was a lot she was willing to do to keep those she loved safe. Blood filled images raced through her mind and she pushed them aside too.

Jorn glanced skywards. "It's time to return to our people. We need to find somewhere safe for them before dark."

Three of the dragons shapeshifted and Amber clambered onto Treon's back again. "Do you have somewhere safe for them to go?"

"Not yet. But we will find another sheltered location in the forest before the day has ended," Treon said.

"How can you be certain?" The forest was vast and

from what she'd seen of it, difficult to find anything in it with how close the trees grew.

"Because we've done it numerous times already."

She tried to figure out the tone she heard in his thoughts. It was either weariness or frustration. She didn't know him well enough to tell which one it might be. She also had no idea what to say to him so she remained silent.

As they neared the camp, Tathen and Cort flew ahead. They returned within minutes, sending their thoughts to all of them before they were in sight. *"The camp was attacked."*

All the dragons picked up speed and Amber clung to Treon. Not that it would be a problem if she fell off him. She could easily shapeshift. But she'd prefer not to fall. She mentally searched ahead. "I can't sense anyone."

"The fight is over?" Treon asked.

She slowly drew in her breath, dreading the need to clarify her words. There were dragons who killed the messenger of bad news and she didn't know any of them here all that well. "I can't sense anyone. Not hybrids and not your people."

"The hunters would have hidden as many as they could." Treon landed in front of the cave.

Amber slid off his back. The ground was torn up in

places and there were dark stains on the ground that took her several seconds to realise was blood. "The place is deserted. No one is hidden."

Jorn crouched by an arrangement of sticks and stones to the side of the entrance of the cave. "They headed this way." He rose to his feet, looking towards his right. "We need to find them."

Amber glanced around the group. Each of them looked worried. "I can help." She frowned as she checked the direction Keeley had gone in. She turned her back on the direction Jorn had indicated. "Your daughter is travelling that way." She gestured in the direction they'd come from, slowly shaking her head as she searched for Caral and discovered she was in a direction partway between the two directions. "Even your sister hasn't gone in the direction Jorn pointed to."

"Where did Caral go?" Morgane asked.

Amber pointed out the direction. "That way."

"How can you know that?" Tathen demanded.

"I made sure I'd be able to find some of you in case I lost track of you." Amber carefully watched each of them, not sure what to expect, ready to turn into a goshawk and take to the skies at the first sign of danger. After this, Ronan was going to owe her. "I don't know this world and have very little idea how to find any of the locations I've been to." But she could easily track down those she had ties to.

"You can find Caral and Keeley," Morgane said.

Amber nodded, still watching them carefully.

"Who is the closest?"

Amber searched for them again. "Caral. She's stopped moving, Keeley hasn't."

Morgane shared a look with Jorn who wrapped his arms around her. "How can we choose?" Morgane demanded.

Amber thought of when she'd directed Crystal to the industrial building Ronan had locked her, Kade, Maira and Brann in. "Maybe you don't. Do you have phones?"

"What is a phone?" Jorn asked.

This world seemed rather medieval, but Amber had thought it worth asking. "A device that lets you talk to people who are a long way from you. Even on the other side of the world."

"You have something like that in your world?" Cort asked.

Amber nodded.

"I wouldn't mind exploring your world one day." Cort glanced at Morgane and Jorn. "Once we make sure Brigitte is no longer a threat."

"How do you talk to people who are a long way from you?" Amber asked.

"Through numerous people who pass along messages," Becan said. "How far is Keeley from here?"

Amber closed her eyes, trying to focus on how far away the half dragon was. She drew in a sharp breath, opening her eyes. "I think she's not far from Brigitte's castle." She had a feeling Keeley was heading towards the castle, but was glad she hadn't said that when she saw the look in Morgane and Jorn's eyes. "She's alive," she hurriedly added.

"What about everyone else?" Tathen asked.

"I'm sorry." Amber wished she had strengthened her ties to all of them. "I didn't think I'd need to know where everyone was."

Becan rested a hand on Morgane's shoulder. "We'll get your daughter back." He glanced at Jorn and Tathen. "And find everyone else."

It didn't take them long to calculate that everyone except Treon would have to go with Morgane. They would be needed to create a long enough communication chain to allow Amber to tell Morgane when she was close to her daughter's location, particularly since her and Treon needed to travel further away from Keeley so they could find

Caral. As soon as Treon was in dragon form, Amber clambered onto his back, directing him where to go. She also regularly told Tathen, who'd been left within her range of mind talking, how close Morgane was to Keeley.

Amber and Treon reached Caral before Morgane reached Keeley. She scrambled off Treon's back the moment he landed, hurrying towards Rainer who was healing a wounded half dragon.

Rainer looked up, his face streaked with almost as much blood as his hands. "They arrived barely an hour after all of you left. We lost two and there are some we haven't been able to find."

Seeing how exhausted Rainer looked, Amber crouched beside his patient, pressing her hands against one of the wounds. "I'll heal those with dragon ancestry." Why hadn't she strengthened her ties to all of them? When she finished helping Rainer she'd have to do something about that.

"Who did we lose?" Treon asked.

Rising to his feet, Rainer gestured towards two bodies lying off to one side.

Treon hurried over to them.

Chapter Eight

Amber kept her attention on the one she healed, not wanting to know who'd died. At least not yet. What if it was Tathen's son? She searched out Morgane's direction, along with Jorn and Keeley's. Jorn remained in the one location and Morgane had nearly reached her daughter. Amber let Tathen know as she moved onto another patient, nodding at the thanks the first patient gave her.

"Have you found everyone else?" Tathen asked as he'd done each time she'd contacted him.

"You'll have to ask Treon." There was no way she was telling him anyone had died. Not when she didn't know who'd died.

"What aren't you telling me?" Tathen demanded.

Amber glanced around the heavily treed area, unable to see everyone due to the vegetation. *"There was a fight. I don't know the names of all those who were injured. You'll have to ask Treon."* She deliberately avoided using the word 'died'. *"Did you pass along the message that Morgane's getting close?"*

"Of course I did."

Amber sighed as she moved onto the next patient, trying not to think of the two who hadn't made it. She really hoped it wasn't Tathen's son. She checked where Morgane was before she turned to Rainer who was healing a hunter. "Why are all of you with Morgane? Wouldn't it be safer to be somewhere else? With someone else. Someone Brigitte isn't interested in coming after."

Rainer looked up from his patient. "Morgane and her family aren't the only ones Brigitte wants dead. All of us here have either offended her, got in her way, or refused to do her bidding at some stage or other. Being elsewhere wouldn't stop Brigitte or her warriors from coming after us."

"So you decided to all gather in one area to make it easier for her to come after you?"

Rainer slowly shook his head. "If only it was that simple. Where would you have us go? Would you have us put other people in danger? And who would you have fight at our side? Someone else for Brigitte to focus her anger on?"

"No, but-" Amber broke off. "Bloody dragons." A

chuckle behind her had her turning her head to see Treon stood nearby. "Is Caral okay?"

Treon nodded. "No worse off than anyone else."

Amber returned the smile of the one she'd finished healing, rising to her feet to face Treon. "She need healing?" She automatically checked where Morgane was, realising the dragon now circled her daughter's location.

"Rainer has already healed her." Treon gave Rainer a nod.

Amber let Tathen know where Morgane was before she spoke aloud to Treon. "Is there somewhere safe we can take everyone? They need shelter." Some of the humans weren't fully recovered from their wounds and those of dragon ancestry weren't much better.

"No." Treon's tone was flat. "There's no place safe from Brigitte. Those who have found safety usually manage it through an elaborate plan to make Brigitte think them dead."

"Is that how your sister escaped?" If it was, why had they trusted her enough to tell her?

He gave a half shrug. "Is anything ever as simple as that?"

Amber couldn't resist grinning, even though there

was very little to be happy about the situation. "You dragons always have to complicate things."

"I'm only half dragon."

"So hunters don't complicate things?"

He chuckled. "I never said that."

Rainer joined them. "We need to get to a safer location before dark."

Amber turned away from them while they discussed places she didn't know. Her gaze was drawn to each of the people she could see. Dirt and blood stained their clothes and streaked their body. They had very few things with them now. She had no idea if their gear had been lost or if they'd hidden it. Hearing Treon raise his voice, she turned back to the two of them. "What do you mean?"

"About?" Treon asked.

"You said Brigitte destroyed a pillar that kept hunters from hiding in the area at your castle before they attacked it," Amber said.

Treon nodded.

"Does that mean she has these pillars, whatever they are, at her castle?" Amber asked.

"Yes," Treon said at the same time as Rainer spoke.

"It's the only way she'd be able to prevent us from bending the light around ourselves and those with us."

"How do you destroy them?" Amber asked.

"It's more than destroying them," Treon said. "You have to find out what they look like and where they've been placed."

Amber replayed his words in her mind. They still didn't make sense. "You don't know what they look like? Didn't you say you had some in your castle?"

Treon laughed softly. "It isn't quite like that. They're metal rods. Most people turn them into a decorative piece in an effort to hide them. Or partially bury them within something else. Even with part of them needing to be open to the air, it can be done in a way to make it hard to spot them."

"So how do you find them? And how did Brigitte find yours?" Amber asked.

"Deceit," Treon said.

"Brigitte sent someone to infiltrate the castle and betray us." Rainer's voice wasn't as sharp as Treon's and there was a sadness to it.

Amber couldn't help wondering if the betrayal had been more personal for Rainer. "Why can't you do the same? Send someone to infiltrate her castle."

"Anyone we'd trust to do that, and not be turned by a bribe from Brigitte, would be known by her," Treon said.

Before Amber could suggest she try and infiltrate the castle, Rainer spoke.

"A few have been suggesting we return to Morgane's castle. It's been long enough that surely her warriors are no longer there."

"No," Treon stated. "If they were hidden, they'd be able to get a message back to Brigitte before we had the chance to stop them."

Amber looked from one to the other. "Maybe not. What if your hunters kept themselves and your warriors invisible until they're all in place to take out whoever might be watching? I could tell you where everyone is."

"There probably isn't anybody watching after all this time," Rainer persisted.

"It's too dangerous." Treon gestured towards those hiding amongst the trees with them. "Haven't they already faced enough today?"

"Then where do you expect them to go?" Rainer demanded.

Treon sighed heavily, his gaze scanning the area. "There has to be somewhere better than that."

"We can't go to any of the villages. Do you want to put friends and family in danger?" Rainer demanded.

Amber wanted to step between them. They didn't

have time for this. "Did you kill the hybrids that came after you?"

Rainer shook his head. "There were too many of them. All we could do was bend the light around us, so they couldn't find us, and run."

"How long do you think we have before they find us?" She mentally searched the area again, as she'd regularly been doing. "There isn't anyone nearby other than your people, but how long do you think it will be before that changes?"

Treon turned his back on them, staring into the forest.

Amber wished she could ask him what he was thinking, but she didn't know him that well. "Who normally makes these decisions?" She moved to the side of him, glancing at him before looking at the same view he stared at. The trees grew close together and would be difficult for dragons to fly amongst. And for wyverns.

"My parents."

"Who makes the decisions when they're not here?"

Treon didn't answer.

Rainer came to stand on the other side of Amber. "The dragons will only take orders from a Gold."

"What about Caral then?" Amber asked.

"Dragons have long memories," Rainer said. "A

few hundred years ago Caral believed Brigitte when she said she wanted to get to know her. That she regretted not having her children in her life."

Treon faced Amber and Rainer. "We'll go to the castle." He nodded towards Amber. "We'll try your suggestion."

"You're not Gold," Amber blurted out. Relief rushed through her when he grinned. She'd thought she was getting better at not saying such things. "I mean-"

Treon interrupted her. "They see me as Gold. I'm both a hunter and a dragon. Something as rare as Gold."

"I'll let everyone know the plan." Rainer strode away from them.

Amber watched him go for a moment before she turned to Treon. "Why do you trust me? How do you know I wasn't faking it when I healed your people?"

"Keeley does."

"Keeley does." She repeated his words. They still made no sense to her. "What does that mean?"

Treon shrugged. "It's difficult to explain. It's like she sees something in people. Not all people. Some she said are impossible to read."

"What did she see in me?"

"A queen."

His words reminded her of Ronan's offer. They sent a shiver down her spine. She had no desire to rule the world. "No. She's mistaken."

Treon smiled briefly. "It's the way she sees people. A King or Queen, an overlord, a jester, a rogue and so many others. Titles that describe what they're like. Not necessarily who they are. Keeley sees a queen as a ruler who is just. Someone who protects their people and makes good choices for them."

Again she felt like she should protest. But she doubted he'd listen. "Is there anything we can do to help everyone get ready?"

"They have their own methods and ways of doing things." He glanced over his shoulder. "Besides, it looks like they're nearly ready."

Amber studied the group of people as they gathered, a man needing to be dragged away from the bodies lying beneath the tree. He protested, wanting to return to the deceased. Amber knew exactly how he felt. The anger and sorrow that competed with each other. It was a pity Ronan had a promise to keep. Ending Brigitte's life would be the safest option. Amber drew in a slow breath, releasing it just as slowly. Once she'd have chosen any other option. She'd obviously been a slow learner.

Sometimes it was the only option when it came to dragons. And knights. The alternative ended in too many deaths. Her gaze was drawn to the bodies beneath the tree. To losing loved ones.

Treon rested a hand on Amber's shoulder. "Are you all right?"

She met his gaze, seeing the concern in his eyes. "I will be." Forcing a smile to her lips, she took a step back from him. "I always am."

He held her gaze a moment longer. "I have trouble believing that. No one is all right all the time."

She had no choice. Too many people relied on her. Shrugging, she glanced at Treon's people. "Looks like they're ready."

Treon studied her, remaining silent. Without saying anything, he shapeshifted, taking to the air once she was on his back. He led the way, eventually going ahead with Amber when they drew close so they could scout the castle.

She remained on his back as he bent the light around them, wishing they could stop for lunch. With all the travelling they'd done it had to be after midday and breakfast felt like it had been ages ago. Trying to ignore her hunger since it was more important to find safety for those with them, she mentally searched the area. There were only two at the front of the castle, a hunter and hybrid who were invisible. It would have been easy to take them out if it hadn't been for the ones she could sense inside and on the battlements. Ones within easy calling distance. There were too many for them to deal with them all at once.

"What can you sense?" Treon asked.

"We need to come up with a better plan."

"What is wrong?" Treon slowed his pace.

"There are too many. We have to come up with a different plan." She refused to lead them into a slaughter. "There must be around fifty people at your castle."

"My parents' castle." Treon landed, becoming human once Amber slipped to the ground. "We have few choices. You've seen what state everyone is in. Are Brigitte's warriors all in the same area?"

"No, but they're hybrids. We barely managed to beat them when we outnumbered them. This time, they'll outnumber us. How many hunters do you have?"

"You're the one who suggested this plan," Treon said. "We need to figure out a way to make it work."

"I didn't think there'd be so many hybrids." Amber searched the area again. They were definitely hybrids. They had that sense of wyverns about them. "It's not just about taking them out, it's about not letting any of them escape so they can let Brigitte know where you are."

"I know. I knew it as soon as you suggested it."

Chapter Nine

Amber was half tempted to ask why Treon had agreed to come here. "What do you want to do?"

Treon stared at her for a moment. "Can you shapeshift into your bird form and sit on my shoulder while I walk through the castle and you tell me where everyone is?"

"It's a goshawk." He made it sound like she was some pirate's parrot.

He grinned fleetingly. "Can you?"

"Yeah." Shifting forms, she flew to his shoulder and landed on it. *"Now what?"*

"Direct me. I need to know where every one of Brigitte's hybrids and hunters are."

"This could take a while," Amber warned.

"Will that be a problem? Can you hold this form that long?"

"I can hold it." She mentally searched the area. *"Okay, you ready to do this?"*

"Yes."

Amber directed him throughout the castle, telling him the location of each hybrid and hunter. The castle itself badly needed repairs. Some of the timber floors in the upper levels were almost burned away and what furniture was left was mostly splinters. The hybrids and hunters appeared to be living on the ground floor and in a few strategic vantage points in the upper levels.

They reached the top of the battlements, standing metres away from where Amber sensed a hybrid and hunter. She shook her head, her feathers ruffling at Treon's suggestion. *"What if we can't take them out before they can call for help?"* And what if she hesitated?

"Then we're far enough away from the other hybrids and hunters that we'll manage to escape before they can reach us." When she didn't reply, he spoke again. "What do you think?"

She thought it was utter madness, but he had a point. *"Okay. The hybrid is on the left and the hunter is on the right."* It was strange not being able to see them, only sense them. It made the thought of taking them out seem less real.

"I'll take the hybrid. This has a good chance of

working. We'll take them from behind." He moved closer to where Amber had told him the hybrid stood.

"How do you know they have their back to us? They could be leaning against the edge of the battlements, not looking out at the forest."

"You don't know Brigitte. None would dare to relax while on guard duty." Treon drew a dagger. "Are you ready?"

"Yeah." Waiting around wasn't going to make the job any easier. It'd only give her time to rethink going ahead with it. She brought to mind the image of the bodies under the tree. The ones they'd had to leave behind, dragging the man from them as he protested them being left in the open. *"I'm ready when you are."*

"Do you wish to shapeshift first?"

"It isn't necessary."

"Are you sure?"

"You sure you're ready?" Amber asked. Maybe she wasn't the only one struggling with this plan.

"Yes. Take them down." As Treon spoke, he took a step forward.

Amber landed behind the hunter as she shapeshifted and drew her sheathed wrist daggers in one fluid movement. She sank them into him. He became visible, his figure taller than her, his wiry body tensing for only a second. Warm blood poured over her hands, the hunter not having had time to move let alone make a sound. He sank to the ground. As she withdrew her daggers, she turned to see Treon had dispatched the hybrid. His opponent had managed to half draw his sword. She stared at the two bodies sprawled out on the battlements.

They both looked so young and very human. And they'd died so quickly. Neither of them had been given a chance to fight back. She couldn't drag her gaze from them, the strong sense of wyvern now gone. She felt like the assassin she'd once thought Ronan was trying to turn her into. Emotions churned within her, all of them muddled, none of them pleasant.

Treon rested his hand on her shoulder. "Are you all right?"

She drew in a shuddering breath, forcing herself not to think about them. She was pretty sure they would have killed her without hesitation if they'd had the chance. Again she brought to mind the bodies under the tree. The ones that had been killed by Brigitte's warriors. She drew in another breath, this one steadier than the last. "Yeah. What are we going to do about the bodies? What if someone discovers them?"

Treon studied her. "Are you sure you're all right?"

"Yeah." Amber stepped away from him, dislodging his hand. She gestured towards the bodies, not looking at them too closely. "What are we going to do with them?"

"There are at least ten others we can use this technique on," Treon said.

"There are forty-six hunters and hybrids left. Are we going to do that with the rest of them?" Her gaze roamed his face, noting all the similarities between him and Ronan. "Getting us killed isn't going to help your people." And she didn't think she could keep doing this. At least not another twenty-three times if he expected her to take out half of them with him.

He stepped forward again, once more resting his hand on her shoulder, his gaze colliding with hers as he lightly squeezed her shoulder. "I think you underestimate your capabilities. There was no hesitation when you attacked Brigitte's hunter. And you didn't let him suffer. You dispatched him swiftly."

She didn't bother telling him he wasn't the first person who'd said she was more capable than she gave herself credit. She also didn't point out that just because she hadn't hesitated the first time didn't mean she wouldn't hesitate the next.

Treon frowned. "Is there something else that's bothering you?"

She wasn't about to share her thoughts with him and let him know exactly how weak she sometimes was. She had no idea how ruthless the dragons could be in this world and if they believed in survival of the fittest like the ones she knew. "We might be caught."

Treon inclined his head. "You're right. My people aren't your people. Our losses aren't yours. I'm sorry. You've helped us more than we could have expected."

"It isn't that. It's just…" Her voice trailed off as she tried to think of a reasonable explanation. She nearly blurted out that she wasn't an assassin.

"If you could direct my people, we'll take them out. Hopefully before they have the chance to kill any more of us."

The image of the bodies under the tree came to her again. "Who were they?"

Again Treon frowned. "Who are you talking about?"

"Your people. The ones who died. Who was the man who didn't want to leave them behind?"

"His wife died. They'd been together nearly fifty years. He has children who'll need to be informed. The other man who died, his brother is one of those missing from when they had to run from the attack.

He's probably dead too. They aren't the first ones we've lost. Over the years we've lost more to Brigitte than to any other cause. She has no sense of family, only self."

She could see the pain in his eyes. The anger. The frustration. The emotions coloured his tone and had him holding his body rigid and caused his hand to tighten on her shoulder. "I'm sorry." She could understand loss. And the fear of it. "I'll help you."

Treon stared at her a moment longer before he nodded. "Thank you. You can't imagine how much this means to us. Most turn away from us when they learn our enemy is Brigitte." A wry smile fleetingly formed. "It's probably a bad idea to let you know considering you're not from this world and have no idea about who are the ones who can cause you the most grief."

A wry smile of her own briefly formed. "You might be surprised by how I feel about your words." If anything, they made her want to fight at his side. She'd always been a sucker for a sob story. More so when those with such a story gritted their teeth and kept going when they had every reason to give up.

"So how do they make you feel?" He stepped even closer.

She was tempted to retreat. He was far too close

and she was worried about another incident like the Alexandre one. That was the last thing she needed. "How about we get this over and done with?" She glanced at the bodies, still trying not to look too closely at them. "Before someone comes and finds them."

Treon inclined his head. "Do you want to ride on my shoulder again? Seems to work well."

Amber shapeshifted in answer, flying to his shoulder. She searched the area, leading the way to the next location, another section of the battlements. They did the same as before, but this time she hesitated, knowing how she felt after the last kill.

The hunter half turned towards her, shock in his brown eyes as she sank her daggers into him. She spun to the side when something touched her on the shoulder, hands raised with balls of fire pooling in them. Seeing it was Treon, she lowered her hands and closed them to extinguish the flames.

"How long has your world been at war?" Treon nodded to her hands that were now at her sides.

"My world isn't at war. At least the part of it where I live isn't."

"I saw how you reacted. Your automatic response was to attack."

"That is from too much time around dragons. You

have a bad habit of wanting what's not yours." Including her. Or at least her abilities as a Dragon Mage. Or alternatively her death so no one else could have the benefit of her abilities.

Treon grinned. "I'm only half dragon."

She had no idea how to respond to that comment, so remained silent.

"Are you ready?"

Amber shapeshifted and landed on his shoulder. She led him to the hunter and hybrid on the next two sides of the battlements. She turned her back on the bodies, trying not to see the brown eyes of the second hunter she'd taken out. They swamped the image of the bodies under the tree. "We can't keep doing this. It will take us too long and we're likely to be caught." She couldn't keep doing this. Couldn't risk the nightmares in a world that she didn't know and wasn't certain of the people. She wanted to believe they could be trusted, but after her many dealings with dragons her trust wasn't so easily given these days.

"It's too much for you I–"

Amber interrupted Treon. "There are two of us and still another forty of them." It might bother her to take their lives, which was an understatement, but she knew one thing about herself for a certainty. She would do whatever it took to make sure that those she cared about would survive. And she couldn't protect them while she was stuck in this world.

"This isn't your fight. I'll understand if-"

Again she interrupted him, her words fierce. "This is my fight. Brigitte took one of mine so she made it my fight."

Treon chuckled. "It seems I'm not the only one with dragon tendencies."

Amber smiled, one that she was pretty sure was similar to Ronan's predatory one. "Apparently I had a good teacher." She didn't add that Ronan thought she was a poor student. Her smile widened when she saw the startled look in Treon's eyes.

"Sometimes I could almost believe you are a dragon." He glanced at the nearby bodies. "Will you continue to help me?"

She wanted to demand if he would help her. If he'd help her rescue Ronan so she could go home to Kade. "While you and I share the same enemy, and I remain in this world, I will fight at your side against her." She didn't want to think about Brigitte being in the dragons' world. Ronan better have a plan for that because she didn't want that dragon let loose where she might harm Kade, Crystal, Rian or the many others she wouldn't want hurt or worse.

Treon inclined his head. "Thank you." He studied her for a moment. "We have another four we can take out before we have to rethink how we do this."

Chapter Ten

Amber shapeshifted into a goshawk and landed on Treon's shoulder. She had no idea what they could do next and worrying about it later didn't seem like the best idea. She was pretty sure Ronan wouldn't have been impressed with that kind of thinking. He probably would have had half a dozen plans lined up before he'd started. She mentally searched the castle and surrounds before directing him to the next two groups. They were outside. One behind the castle and one out the front. She tried not to think about how high her kill count was becoming. Bloody dragons. She also tried not to think of brown eyes filled with surprise.

"I'll call the hunters close. Each of them can hide two others."

Amber stared at him for a moment. "Why are

Brigitte's hybrids and hunters only in groups of two? Why don't the hunters hide two hybrids?"

"Hybrids can only work together for short periods of time. They're too temperamental and end up fighting each other instead of doing the task they've been set." Treon chuckled. "We've been able to use that to our advantage quite a few times."

Amber slowly shook her head. "Why didn't you tell me this earlier? I thought we'd only have eight, not twelve, when it was time for them to attack. That will make a difference." She mentally searched the area again. "Oh no."

"What's wrong?" Treon demanded.

"There's a hunter and hybrid headed towards each of the ones we've taken out."

"It must be time for them to swap guards. We can use this to our advantage. You can direct all of us to them so we can take them out before they see the dead warriors and while they're away from the rest of those stationed here. I'll bring the other hunters into our conversation."

Before Amber could protest, four others joined the conversation, including Rainer. The three she didn't know each said their name. Rakel, Jannik and Devan. She directed each of them to go after the separate groups of hunters and hybrids. There was still a hunter and hybrid no one was going after. They were headed towards the ones that had been guarding the front of the Castle.

Scanning the nearby area and finding it was clear, Amber flew through the nearest window. *"Take out the hybrid first, Treon. They seem to be the hardest one to fight."*

"That's what you think," Treon thought back to her.

She wasn't sure if he was joking so she concentrated on telling them where they needed to go as she flew towards the two approaching the dead bodies out the front. She flew down to land behind the hybrid, shape shifting and drawing her wrist daggers as she landed. He was facing her and had half drawn his sword. She didn't hesitate this time, plunging her daggers in. One ended up in his side and the other angled up under his ribs.

He drew the dagger out of his stomach and tossed it aside, managing to finish drawing his sword.

Amber drew out the other dagger, trying not to worry about the wild look in his eyes, his roar ringing out loudly. There was no way anyone could have missed hearing that. She dodged his attack, throwing several fireballs at him.

The hunter joined the attack, using her magic to send a gust of air at Amber, knocking her off her feet. The hunter readied a bow and arrow, aiming at Amber.

She rolled out of the way, the arrow striking the ground where she'd been. Surging to her feet, she sheathed her dagger and shapeshifted into a panther. She leapt at the hybrid, bringing him to the ground, going for the throat. Warm blood filled her mouth and she spat it out when she shapeshifted into her human form, throwing herself at the hunter who'd readied another arrow.

The hunter forced a gust of air at Amber.

Ready for it this time, Amber threw herself to the side, becoming a goshawk she landed behind the hunter, drawing her dagger and stabbing the hunter in the back.

The hunter dropped her bow, sagging against Amber, her breath jagged with pain. "You've killed my children too. Brigitte has imprisoned them at Cliffview. If I fail my task, she'll have them killed."

"You lie." Amber wanted to beg the woman to tell her every word was a lie.

"The oldest is six." Her words were soft, barely loud enough to be heard.

Amber struggled to hold up the hunter's weight. "Six?" Her voice had a high pitched panicked tone that she hadn't heard in a long time.

"My daughters will have no one," the hunter breathed out the words, blood staining her and Amber.

An arrow came towards them and Amber realised the rest of Treon's people had joined the fight while she'd been preoccupied with the hunter. She didn't have time to think, only react. She dragged the hunter to the side, trying to heal her as she drew out the dagger, following her to the ground.

The woman made a pained sound as she landed face first on the ground, weakly struggling.

Amber feared it was impossible until she realised there was some dragon blood in the hunter. Enough she could heal her. Amber didn't know if it was due to the woman being a hunter or the types of dragons in this world, but with how little dragon blood was in the woman, she wouldn't have normally have been able to heal someone.

The hunter turned her head to the side. "Why?"

"Tell me what you mean. Is it the same for everyone? Do you all work for Brigitte unwillingly?" Amber demanded.

"Why are you healing me? I can't let you live," the hunter said.

"Tell me about Brigitte. Are all her people captives?" The flow of blood stopped as Amber continued to heal the hunter, keeping her pinned against the ground.

"No. When she sent hybrids to capture our village, some were happy to be her people."

"Why would they be?" Amber finally finish healing the hunter, rolling her over to study her face. Dirt and blood were smeared across her skin and light brown hair, her brown eyes filled with pain and worry. Amber's heart sank. The hunter was telling the truth. She tried not to think about the other brown eyes. Had he been willing or had he served Brigitte against his will?

"Some serve her because she's given them the power they couldn't earn on their own." The hunter met Amber's gaze. "I can't let you live." There was regret in her voice. "As wrong as it feels to repay you that way, I have no choice. Not if I want my kids to live."

"If you want your kids to have a chance, you won't keep attacking me," Amber warned.

"Letting you live won't help them. The only thing that can help them is if I never disappoint Brigitte. Ever."

Amber grinned, a touch of Ronan's predatory smile in it. "Are you sure? Brigitte is going down. Will you and your children go down with her?" She saw the uncertainty in the hunter's eyes. "I'm not from your world. I have abilities and knowledge that those from your world don't have."

"She has an army far larger than anyone else in this country. Probably even larger than any one group of the savages. And the hybrids are more fierce than other warriors."

Amber didn't relax her grip on the hunter even though the uncertainty in her eyes was now in her tone. "I'm Amber. What's your name?"

"You can't win against her and the hybrids no matter what world you're from."

"What is your name?" Amber asked again.

"Gunsa. Knowing it won't make a difference."

"Call your hunters, Gunsa. Tell them to surrender. All the hybrids are dead. We can defeat Brigitte and her warriors."

"It's too late. You can't stop her from learning what happened here. There's a hybrid who lives in the forest between here and the castle. He's been told of the attack. He'll fly straight to the castle and tell Brigitte everything. One of her loyal hunters told him before your people killed him."

Amber searched the area between the two castles. She could find only one hybrid. She mentally reached for Treon. *"I need your help."*

"I'm busy with this hunter who's trying to kill me."

She smiled at the dry tone to his thoughts before speaking aloud to Gunsa. "Either we kill all of you or you surrender. Either way, Brigitte will think you've failed. Surrendering will give you a chance to save your children."

"You expect me to trust you after you tried to kill me?" Gunsa struggled to escape.

"You are holding the castle of my allies. Did you think Brigitte's attack on this place would go unpunished?"

"No one goes against her."

Again Amber smiled. "Don't they?" If it was one thing she'd learned about surviving amongst dragons, it was to never show weakness and always retaliate. She didn't know what hunters were like, but they obviously spent a lot of time amongst dragons. "I have survived Hell Hounds, assassins, Elders and attacks from some of the oldest dragons. And I haven't lost." She didn't dare lose. There were too many counting on her. "And I'm not about to lose now."

"Would you promise to swear that you captured us rather than we surrendered if it turns out that Brigitte is the one enemy you can't win against?"

"I will offer to do that for you and the three hunters that still live if you surrender immediately."

The hunter didn't answer straight away. "We surrender."

Amber rose to her feet, holding out a hand to the hunter. She drew Gunsa to her feet. "Where is Cliffview?" After collecting her dagger, and sheathing it, she held up a hand when Gunsa started to speak, Treon now talking to her.

"All the hunters have vanished. Can you direct us to where they are?"

Amber automatically searched for them, about to tell Treon they had surrendered. She spoke to Gunsa instead. "All of you. I expect the one leaving to surrender as well." She sent her thoughts to Treon next. *"I'll meet everyone at the front of the castle."*

"You can tell where we are?" Gunsa stared at her, shock in her tone.

Amber's lips again curved into an imitation of Ronan's predatory smile. "Did you think you could trick me? Tell them to come back. Immediately." She noticed the hunter was now headed towards her.

"He was going after the hybrid," Gunsa said. "He wasn't trying to escape."

Amber turned to face Treon who she could sense behind her, coming closer. "Look after things here and see that the hunters don't come to harm. They're my prisoners. And in my world, we have laws about how prisoners should be treated." She tried not to think about the time she'd been Wayne and Vikki's prisoner. "I'll be back soon." She glanced around the area, her gaze momentarily resting on each of her prisoners even though she couldn't see them. "All of you hunters can stop hiding. And don't try to escape." She strengthened her ties to each of them. "I will track you down and you won't like that at all."

"Where are you going?" Treon asked.

Amber kept track of Brigitte's warrior. "I have a hybrid to catch before he can carry tales to Brigitte."

Treon rested a hand on her shoulder. "I'll go with you. Surely you don't think you can take on a hybrid and win."

She dredged up a smile, trying to ignore the fear she felt at facing a hybrid alone. "Of course I do. I'll see you soon." She leapt into the air, becoming a goshawk and streaking through the forest. She stayed below the treeline, her smaller form making it easy to weave through the vegetation. She slowly gained on the hybrid who seemed to be remaining at a steady pace. As long as she stayed in cover, he wouldn't know she was after him until the last second. She didn't know exactly how she was going to stop him.

She had her magic, daggers and claws. That would have to be enough.

Staying in cover, Amber kept mentally searching the area, worried about how close they were getting to the castle. She forced herself to go faster. She didn't know if Gunsa had told the truth about her children, and the children of other hunters, but she wasn't about to risk Brigitte killing off the families of the hunters she'd forced to serve her. Everything she'd learned about the dragon made her fear she might not be capable of taking her down no matter what she said. Not that it would stop her. Brigitte had Ronan who was not only her ally, but her only way home. He was also family as far as she was concerned.

She waited until she was below the hybrid before she flew up past him to land on his back and become human. She threw two fireballs at his wings before she was flung from his back when he rolled in the air to dislodge her. Becoming a goshawk, she flew at his face, landing on his back when he angled away to avoid her attacks. Again she turned human. This time she used a dagger to slice into the membranes of one of his wings. She barely had the chance to slice them twice before she was thrown from his back, sheathing the dagger as she plummeted towards the trees.

It took her a few seconds before she could

shapeshift, pain filling her from the force of his action when he'd thrown her from him. This time when she tried to land on his back, he immediately went into a roll. She'd obviously use that technique too many times. Aiming for his wings, she used her claws and beak, mentally blocking him when he tried to force his way into her mind. She had no interest in anything he had to say.

She continued to aim for his wings until he faltered. She landed on his back again, becoming human so she could use her dagger on the wings. She threw herself from his back when he plummeted towards the trees below. Becoming a goshawk, she flew after him. He crashed through the canopy, the branches of the closely packed trees keeping him from dying from the fall.

Landing on the ground in front of him, she became human, as he had done. Drawing her sword, she faced him, surprised he hadn't taken more damage in the fall. She blocked his attack, the force of it radiating through her arm, and dodged the next attack. There was no way she could fight him like this. He was still too strong. Dodging again, she sheathed her sword and became a goshawk. Flying above him, she swooped down to land behind him in human form. She didn't have time to draw her daggers before he was facing her. Again she became a goshawk, flying up out of his reach.

Darting in, she raked her claws across his face, leaving bloody scratches behind. Diving to the side, she barely escaped being hit by his sword. This wasn't working. Flying upwards, she landed on a solid tree branch, becoming human and throwing two fireballs at him. Losing her balance, she shapeshifted and flew towards another tree where she landed again.

The hybrid roared, throwing himself at the base of the tree.

Chapter Eleven

Amber clung to the trunk as the tree swayed back and forth. It was impossible to throw any fireballs at the hybrid. Letting go, she became a goshawk as she tumbled towards the ground, pulling up at the last second and angling away from the hybrid. She swooped down behind him, flying around him as he spun to face her. Landing, she became human and managed to draw her daggers and sink them into his back. Before he could finish turning, she pulled the daggers out of his back and sheathed them before again heading skywards.

The hybrid roared, staggering as blood ran down his back, mingling with that of his other wounds. "You won't get away with this. Brigitte will hunt you down."

She didn't bother answering, kept attacking instead. Now he'd slowed considerably she tried her sword, cutting his arm and side. Still, he kept coming at her. Darting out of reach of his sword, she sheathed her own, repeatedly throwing fireballs at him. He staggered as each one struck, continuing to advance on her. She retreated, continuing to throw fireballs. He was as hard to kill as a Hell Hound. And in some ways he reminded her of them.

He threw himself at her, roaring as another fireball struck him.

Amber stumbled backwards, tripping on a fallen log.

The hybrid landed on her, his hands wrapping around her throat.

She tried to pull his hands away. His grip tightened, making it hard for her to breathe. Pressing her hands against his wrists, and the wide metal band that went around one of them, she forced fireballs into him. The edges of her vision was going dark and she feared she'd pass out, when the metal band snapped open and with a roar, he let go of her and took to the sky.

Gasping and coughing, Amber rolled onto her side before struggling to her feet, mentally searching the area for the hybrid. Finding him, she tried to figure out what was different about him. He seemed more wyvern than human now. Her gaze was drawn to the metal band. She needed to figure out more about them. If it was the same as the one on Ronan, then she now had a way to remove it. Later though. Right now she needed to deal with the hybrid. Before he could make his way to Brigitte.

Becoming a goshawk, she took to the sky, mentally searching the area. Other than her and the hybrid, there were no others nearby. She angled away from the castle, following the hybrid. What was he doing? Wasn't he meant to be taking a message to Brigitte? She reached for his mind, barely catching a glimpse of anger and chaos before he blocked her. He was a completely different person.

She continued to fly after him, ideas racing through her mind. The hybrids were Brigitte's advantage. What would she have left without them? She really needed to find out more information so she could come up with a decent plan. She didn't want to be stuck in this world forever. Plans would have to wait. Right now, she had to catch the hybrid. Just because he wasn't going directly to the castle, didn't mean he wouldn't eventually let Brigitte know what had happened.

It didn't take long to catch up with him since although his wings had healed some, it wasn't enough for him to fly as well as he normally could. Like before, she went for the wings. They were soon in the same state as they'd been in earlier. She also needed to move quicker this time and take him down before he had the chance to heal. Particularly with how fast he could heal. She didn't know if that was typical of the wyverns in this world or if it was something to do with him being a hybrid.

The moment he landed on the ground, shapeshifting, she dived after him, landing behind him. Becoming human, she drew her daggers to sink them into him before he had the chance to turn. This time, she heard his heartbeat slow and when she withdrew the daggers, he sank to the ground, his heartbeat coming to a stop. She stared down at him, surprised that the final attack had been so easy compared to the earlier fight. He remained human. She'd half expected him to become a wyvern in death. She had so many questions to ask Treon. She stared at her bloody daggers before she sheathed them. It was no point in worrying about cleaning them when her wrist sheathes were already a mess from the amount of times she'd already sheathed them while fighting. Shapeshifting, she took to the sky again. Exhaustion tugged at her, but she refused to give into it as she turned and headed back to Treon and his people.

As she flew, she searched out all those that she knew in this world. Keeley was now next to Ronan, close enough they were likely in the same room. They hadn't been that close earlier. Possibly, there'd been an entire castle between them. She was surprised to find Morgane and those with her, were now headed towards Treon. She again checked where Keeley was. Surely they hadn't given up on rescuing their daughter. She supposed she'd soon find out. Making a detour to where she'd fought the hybrid, she scooped up the metal band in her claws and headed towards Treon.

She arrived not long after Morgane and her companions, shapeshifting and entering the front door of the castle to find everyone in the foyer, arguing. Someone demanded the prisoners be killed while another suggested trading them for Keeley.

Morgane interrupted them partway through the suggestion. "That would only work if Brigitte cared for someone other than herself. But she doesn't. There has only ever been one person Brigitte has cared about."

"I still say we should kill the hunters." One of the dragons glared at Gunsa and her companions who remained off to one side, Treon standing beside them.

Amber stepped forward. "They are my prisoners. They surrendered to me. No one is to harm them."

"You weren't here watching them," the same dragon stated.

Amber took a step towards him, tossing the metal band onto the floor at his feet. "No, I was chasing after the hybrid who was trying to reach Brigitte and let her know what has happened here. Would you have preferred I let him get away so I could stay here and guard my prisoners?"

Treon picked up the metal band. "Where did you get this?"

"Off the hybrid."

Morgane took the metal band from her son. "How did you unlock it?"

Amber smiled. There were some things she planned to keep to herself. She nodded towards the metal band. "How does it work? Why does she put them on her hybrids?"

"To control them," Morgane said.

"How?" Amber needed more information than anyone seemed interested in giving her. She turned to Gunsa. "Surely you know how they work."

Gunsa shook her head. "It's a closely guarded secret. Only her hunter, the one that's been with her for centuries, knows how to make them and exactly how they work. All we know is that if a hybrid doesn't wear them, then they're more aggressive than usual and want to kill everything in sight. Even allies. They are more wyvern than human."

Amber smiled, remembering turning dragons feral with her brother. "If I remove the metal bands, then left the area, the hybrids could take down the enemy for us."

"How do you remove them?" Gunsa asked. "It's not meant to be possible without the word Brigitte has used to lock them."

"How do we know that one wasn't faulty?" one of the prisoners asked.

"The dead still wear theirs," Treon said.

Amber nodded. She wanted to make sure it hadn't been a fluke as much as the rest of them wanted to be certain of it. Once a dead hybrid was dropped at her feet, she crouched beside him and wrapped her hands around the band. She pushed fireballs into it, barely any space for them to form, the metal heating as she held onto it. Just when she started to think it wouldn't break, it snapped open. Letting go of the band, she watched as it dropped to the floor. She looked up at those crowding in around her, grinning at them. "Happy?"

Gunsa stared at Amber. "What are you?"

"A Dragon Mage." She rose to her feet, maintaining eye contact with Gunsa.

"I've never heard of them before," Gunsa said.

"None of us have." Morgane glanced around at everyone. "But we can use this." She paused a moment. "Somehow."

"We have other things to do first." Becan stepped forward, organising people to keep watch on the battlements and others to go hunting. Still others were sent to assess the condition of the castle and find them somewhere to stay. Four of them were sent to take the hunters to the dungeons.

Amber stepped between Gunsa and the half dragon who would have led her away. "Not this one. I have questions for her."

He glanced at Morgane, who nodded, before stepping back from Amber and Gunsa.

Morgane remained silent until only her, Jorn, Becan, Cort, Treon, Gunsa and Amber were in the foyer. She turned to Gunsa. "Does Brigitte expect you to send messages to keep her informed of what happens here?"

Gunsa glanced at Amber, not answering.

"Do you know if any messages are sent?" Amber asked.

"I know how things are run here," Gunsa said.

Amber tried to keep the frustration out of her voice. "Why won't you tell us then?"

Gunsa glanced at Morgane. "I don't trust her. Everyone knows the two of them hate each other."

"I don't hate her," Morgane said. "I wish I did."

Amber's jaw tightened. Taking a deep breath, she slowly let it out before speaking. "We're your only chance of saving your children."

"Mine aren't the only ones she's holding captive," Gunsa said.

Morgane looked between the two of them. "What is going on?"

Amber explained what Gunsa had told her earlier. "Where is Cliffview?"

"Not far from Brigitte's castle. Maybe an hour. Just out of the snow. In the warmer months, they grow food for those at her castle," Morgane said.

"So if we helped them escape, she'd have no food for her warriors," Amber said.

"She has enough stored up to get her through at least a year and could always send them to raid different areas," Gunsa said. "There are also two other villages. We're not the only one."

"If you're sent out to fight for her, then who is doing the farming?" Amber asked.

"My husband and our children all work one of the farms, along with my parents and siblings. Not everyone is forced to fight for her. But at least one member from every family is." Gunsa met Amber's gaze. "About eighty percent of the hunters who fight for her are forced to do so due to their families being held captive."

"What is stopping them from leaving the villages?" Amber asked.

"Hybrids. There is easily thirty of them at each village, sometimes more if there have been any problems," Gunsa said.

Amber really wished she could talk to Ronan. He was the one good at plotting and planning. She was an amateur in comparison.

"What are you considering doing?" Morgane asked Amber. "And where does Keeley fit into your plans? I'm not about to leave my daughter with Brigitte. Her life won't be very long if I do that."

Jorn slipped an arm around Morgane's waist, drawing close to her as his gaze met Amber's. "None of us will leave her there. We'd never turn our back on one of our people let alone our daughter."

Amber looked from one to the other, barely managing not to smile as an idea formed. "I'll check on her." It'd hopefully give her a chance to talk to Ronan and get his ideas on what they should do. After all, he was the one who'd got them into this mess.

"What about my children?" Gunsa demanded. "You were the one who offered to rescue them."

Amber stepped forward so there were only centimetres separating her and Gunsa. "I always honour my word." The world she was a part of wouldn't allow anything else of her.

"I know nothing of you." Gunsa unwaveringly met her gaze. "Only fools give their complete trust to another."

"I don't want your complete trust. I only need you to believe I'll do what I say I will. Good or bad. Whether you like it or not. Before we rescue anyone, we need to find out more about what is going on at Brigitte's castle." And she needed to talk to Ronan. "Rushing in without all the details is only going to get everyone killed." Not that she always followed that advice if it was someone she loved who was in danger.

"I'll go with you to the castle," Morgane said.

Amber turned to face her. "No."

"It's my daughter who's in danger," Morgane protested.

"Exactly. Would you wait if you thought you had an opportunity to rescue her even if that opportunity only had a slim chance of success?" Amber asked.

"I'm not about to leave-"

Amber interrupted Morgane. "You're not coming with me. If you want my help, then I won't have you at my side when I go to Brigitte's castle." She couldn't risk it. From what she'd seen of Morgane, she'd do anything to save her daughter. Even putting herself in danger. Much like she would be willing to do. Which meant she had a good idea of what could go wrong from experience.

Cort and Becan both moved to stand one on either side of Morgane. It was Cort who spoke while Becan placed his hand against Morgane's back. "Do you think you can stop us from going after one of our own?"

Chapter Twelve

Amber raised her chin, refusing to let any of them see her worries and fears. Being outnumbered in a strange world wasn't a good position to be in. "How many years have you been trying to take Brigitte down?"

"You think you can come to our world and take over, completing the task we've been unable to complete?" Becan's tone was surprisingly mild.

Amber studied him for a moment, certain his feelings weren't as mild as his tone from the look she could see in his eyes. He was very much a dragon and Keeley was his. She knew exactly how possessive dragons were. Dredging up the smile that mimicked Ronan's predatory one, she took a step towards Becan. "I guess only time will tell. Now I will expect you to take care of my prisoners while I'm gone."

"We haven't agreed to let you go without us,"

Morgane said. "There is nothing preventing us from going after Keeley without you."

"I have the ability to see your enemy when they're hidden." Amber glanced at Treon. "As I've already told your son, I'll fight at your side while I'm in this world and as long as we share the same enemy. I'm not about to leave Ronan with her."

"You can't expect us to trust you. None of us know you," Cort protested.

"Keeley trusts her," Treon said.

His words brought silence and from the way they all looked between Morgane and Jorn, and occasionally to one of the others, Amber assumed they were arguing amongst themselves. She wanted to demand they speak aloud, but she was already pushing things by refusing to take Morgane with her.

Treon turned to Amber. "I'll go with you." He smiled. "I trust you. Just like Keeley does."

"She has been wrong before," Becan said.

"Not for decades. She understands her ability now," Treon said.

Gunsa glanced at each of them. "No wonder you've never triumphed against Brigitte. You make your decisions based on emotions. She'll always win. She has no one she cares about enough to have them used against her."

Amber stared at Gunsa, ideas slowly forming. Her lips curved into a smile that eventually widened into a grin. "You're wrong."

"No, I'm not," Gunsa stated. "I've seen her kill warriors, her own warriors, when someone offered to trade them to her for one of her prisoners. Then turn around and have the prisoners killed in front of their loved ones."

For a moment she worried that Ronan might consider becoming Brigitte's ally. Someone willing to do whatever it took to win sounded like a person he'd admire. But she'd captured him and made it impossible for him to shapeshift or use any of his abilities. He'd never forgive her for that. "She needs the hunter who makes the metal bands."

Gunsa glanced at the band that Treon held. "She has thousands of them and they can be used over and over again."

Amber took the band from Treon. "How does it work?"

"You place it on someone and whisper a word against it." Treon took it back from her, putting it on his wrist and snapping it closed. He held his hand out to her. "Shall we see if it still works?"

Morgane pulled away from Jorn and Becan. "No. Treon, what are you thinking?"

Treon continued to hold his hand out to Amber, meeting her gaze as he answered his mother. "That we need to know what to expect."

Amber took hold of his hand, bending her head to whisper Kade's name against the band. She missed him so much. And with everything that was going on in this world, it looked like it'd be ages before she could return to her own world. She looked up at Treon when he stepped close.

"I feel no different." Treon's voice was soft as he leaned in close to her.

Amber let go of his hand to take a step back, regretting the action when she saw the look in his eyes. She nearly blurted out that she had more than enough dragons in her life and had no need of another one. "Can you remove the band?"

Treon opened the band, letting it fall to the floor between them. He grinned at her. "Want to try shackling me again?"

She nearly took another step back from him. She held her ground, meeting his gaze. "I think we know all we need to know now."

He lowered his voice further. "Not even close."

Amber fought the urge to look away. "If you're coming with me I'm leaving as soon as I've had something to eat."

"I'll join you for your meal." He smiled. "I'll see what I can organise for us."

He was gone before she could protest. It wasn't his offer of food that she wanted to protest, but the way he'd invited himself to join her. It looked like she'd need to tell him that she wasn't likely to ever be interested in him. An image of Kade filled her mind. The word 'mine' instantly came to mind, followed by a fierce feeling. Somehow she'd find a way to return home. She turned to Gunsa. "Do hybrids heal quicker than wyverns?"

"No." Gunsa glanced at the metal band on the floor at Amber's feet. "It's the magic in the bracelet. It has a healing power placed on it. Not a strong one, but enough to keep them fighting past the point most warriors would be capable of."

"Then I need to make sure I remove them each time I face one of her hybrids."

"There are thousands of them," Gunsa warned.

Amber mimicked Ronan's predatory smile. "I've always loved a challenge." She nearly laughed when Gunsa took a step back from her. Obviously she was getting better at the smile with all the practice she'd had using it.

"You'll find plenty of challenges around here,"

Becan said before facing Gunsa. "You will have to go in the dungeons with your fellow hunters."

Gunsa inclined her head. "I expected that."

Amber stepped between Gunsa and Becan. "You will treat them well and see that they're fed and none of them are to be harmed." She would check out the dungeons later. She wasn't about to have any of them go through what she'd been through.

"I will see to it." Becan led Gunsa away.

"Will you give Keeley a message from me?" Morgane asked. "Brigitte put one of her bracelets on her so we couldn't contact her."

"I'll try." She had no idea how close she'd be able to get to Ronan or Keeley. A goshawk wasn't exactly the ideal form in which to sneak around in a castle. What she needed was one that no one would think twice about. Maybe a house cat or something similar. Not that she knew how many different animals it was possible for her to learn how to shift into.

"Tell her to do whatever she has to in order to survive. We'd rather her live than have her avoid harming another because she was worried about how it'd affect me," Morgane said.

Amber stared at Morgane for a moment. Had she just given her daughter permission to kill her own grandmother? She had no idea, but it was the only thing that made sense. "I'll try."

"Thank you." Morgane paused a moment. "Treon has a meal ready for the two of you. I'll show you to where he is." She glanced at her companions, giving a slight shake of her head.

Amber walked at Morgane's side, glancing over her shoulder at Jorn and Cort who watched them walk away. She waited until they should be out of hearing before she spoke. "You wanted to speak to me alone?"

Morgane laughed softly. "It was that obvious?"

Amber shrugged.

"I wanted to speak about Treon."

"What about him?"

"You'll return to your world after this," Morgane said.

"Yes." Her life was there. Those she loved and the places that were important to her. And so too were her enemies.

"He seems very interested in you."

Amber started to protest, changing her mind. "There's nothing for him to be interested in."

"Have you told him that?"

"Once." And obviously she'd need to tell him again.

"My family has suffered more than their fair share of pain over the centuries."

She didn't doubt it when they had someone like Brigitte wanting them dead. "I'm sorry for your many losses."

Morgane stopped to face Amber, placing a hand on her upper arm. "Some losses are almost impossible to recover from."

Pain burst through her at the memory of being told Kade had died.

"I see you know what I mean."

"More than I wish." She held Morgane's gaze. "I'll do all I can to see that your daughter lives."

"And Treon? Don't let him do anything stupid in an effort to save his sister. He, more than the others, has that dragon possessiveness. He would fight to the death for any he cared for. Even if that feeling wasn't returned."

Again she wanted to protest. She liked him, but didn't love him with the overwhelming feeling she had for Kade. Or even care about him in the way she cared for her brother or her best friend. Or even her first warrior. There wasn't much she wouldn't do to protect Jay, Crystal and Rian. "I will do everything I possibly can to protect them and return them to you."

Morgane's hand momentarily tightened on her

arm. "Why?" She visibly swallowed. "I know I should be happy that you're willing to help and not question it, but I can't help wondering what your motives are."

Ronan would have said she was an easy mark when it came to a sad story. But it was more than that. "Treon welcomed me to your world. I have only one person here and he's being held against his will by a common enemy." Although she had to wonder exactly how much it was against his will with what he'd said to her when she'd last spoken to him. "It'd be pretty lame to stab him in the back after what he's done for me."

"You have integrity."

She had no idea how to reply to that comment. A shrug seemed like the wrong response and every comment she came up with seemed either insulting or mocking.

Morgane smiled. "You don't take compliments well, do you?"

Amber chuckled. "Apparently not."

Morgane lowered her hand. "I'll show you to where Treon is so you can eat before you leave."

"Thanks."

The meal was mostly silent, consisting of bread, venison and apples. It was a strange combination, but Amber was hungry enough to eat almost anything.

Even willing to hunt down her own meal and eat it raw if that was what it took.

After they'd eaten, Treon led the way outside, nodding in reply to the few people they passed who wished him luck. "Thank you for letting me accompany you."

Amber stepped outside of the castle. "You do know nothing has changed."

He glanced at her. "About what?"

"One day I'll return home to my friends and family. And to Kade."

"That is the name of the one you love?"

"Yeah."

He studied her a moment. "What is it about him that had you falling in love with him?"

Amber laughed. "Love is not rational." She was pretty certain most human emotions were irrational, messy and sometimes downright insane.

"You do love him."

She laughed again at his tone. "Yeah. I'd kill anyone who harmed him."

"You say that like you'd say you'd make a meal for him. Like it's something ordinary and common."

She stopped walking and turned to face him. "There is nothing ordinary about it. Messy and bloody are the words that come to mind." She couldn't help thinking about Vikki and plunging the dagger into her.

"You've killed someone for harming him."

Chapter Thirteen

Amber met Treon's gaze, trying to figure out the emotion she saw in their depths. "It wasn't pretty." She'd been consumed with pain and anger, believing Kade dead.

"I envy him."

She couldn't miss the depth of the emotions in his voice. Her lips slowly curved into a smile. "I wouldn't if I was you. There's probably been more than a few times when he's wondered what he's got himself into."

Treon laughed. "I'm sure there has been. You seem to have a rather strong personality."

Amber's smile became a grin. "That's one way of putting it. My grandmother doesn't put it quite so nicely."

Treon's smile faded at the word 'grandmother'. "We should go."

She felt like she should apologise. "Ronan has promised to return Brigitte to her world. Soon she won't be a problem for you."

"Do you really want her in your world?"

"Not at all, but a promise is binding."

"I would travel to your world with you if it comes to that point."

"Why?"

"She isn't your problem. She's ours. As much as I'd like to forget about her and no longer worry about what she might do, I don't turn away from my responsibilities. Nor do my parents or siblings."

"A pity the Golds of this world don't know how to use the Void."

"I've heard tales of it from my mother and also from Gilda before she left with my sister."

"I wonder if a Pliethin would work on you since you're different. Both hunter and dragon."

"None of us know how to use one."

"Then I guess that's something we need to take care of." Amber grinned. Maybe Ronan might not be her only way home. She wouldn't leave him here though, but if she could travel home, she could bring back help. And they certainly needed it.

"Hunter children catch them and put them in glass jars. It takes more skill than catching fireflies.

Although their parents make them wear dragon-leather gloves as they worry what touching them might do to their children."

Amber started to reassure him that they only effected Gold dragons and those with either the blood or bone of a Gold in their system. She remained silent. Who knew how a Pliethin might change someone in this world. Sensing Morgane headed towards them, Amber glanced over her shoulder. The dragon wasn't in sight yet. "We should go."

Treon nodded before shapeshifting. *"What did my mother have to say to you earlier?"*

"What makes you think she said anything to me?" Amber clambered up onto his back, again wishing she had a saddle.

"She walked with you alone. It's rare that she's alone."

"She worries about you."

Treon launched himself into the sky. *"She worries about all of us far too much. Brigitte's actions aren't her responsibility."*

"Why does she feel that way?"

"Because she had the chance to go after Brigitte when she was weak and she didn't take it. None of us blame her. Brigitte is her mother. We wouldn't have expected her to kill her mother. I'd kill Brigitte before I allowed Mum to do so."

"She's your grandmother."

"No, she's my enemy. The woman who has killed many of the people I've cared about and hunted those I love. If it wasn't for Mum's feelings on the subject, I'd have gone after her decades ago."

Amber had no idea what to say in reply so she remained silent, leaning forward against him. The air was cold at this height and even with her warmer clothes, it still made her wish for the warmer climate of home. When she did go home, she would convince Kade to go somewhere warm and tropical with her. Maybe the Whitsundays. Long sunny days on white beaches soaking in the warmth as she thawed out after being constantly taken into the snow-covered mountains.

As they drew close to the castle, Treon made them invisible, heading towards the window of the castle Amber directed him to. Sensing both Brigitte and Ronan in the room, she became a goshawk and had Treon leave her on the roof while he retreated a distance, first making her promise to call him if she had any problems.

She perched on the edge of the roof in goshawk form, the snow making her feet feel frozen. Finding a more secure location, she lay down, becoming a panther, hoping her fur would help with the cold. It helped, but not as much as she'd hoped. She searched the area, checking where everyone was, noticing a small cat running along one of the corridors after a mouse. It reminded her of her earlier thoughts. Focusing on those nearby, she found that there were only two. None of Brigitte's warriors was in the area.

Brigitte was with Ronan, the two of them very close together. Listening for a moment, she realised Brigitte was asking him about Pliethins. Did Brigitte plan to learn how to use one? She dreaded the thought of this dragon being able to travel between and throughout the worlds. They had to deal with her before she reached that point.

Brigitte moved away from Ronan. "I'll see you again this evening."

"I have no plans to go anywhere," Ronan said.

Brigitte laughed. "That is a little difficult to do since you're chained to my bed."

Ronan chuckled. "You've always underestimated me, Bri."

Brigitte moved close to Ronan again. "Tell me, how you could escape while you're wearing one of my bracelets and are chained?"

There was silence. Amber wished Brigitte would hurry and leave so she could get in out of the cold.

Brigitte again moved away from Ronan. "It's very

tempting to spend the rest of the afternoon in here with you, but I have someone to interrogate."

"Remember your promise," Ronan said.

"I never promised anything. Only said I'd think about it." Brigitte now stood at the door.

Amber wanted to tell Ronan to stop talking and let her go.

"And I've told you I'd keep my original promise, even though you keeping me chained up negates any need for me to do so, if you'll give me the chance to learn what these hunter-dragons are like."

"You've already had a couple of hours to talk to her and have learned nothing. Now it's my turn."

When Brigitte started to walk away, Amber wanted to protest. What were the two of them planning? Did Ronan know Keeley was his granddaughter? Would that make a difference to him? When Brigitte kept moving away from the room, Amber shifted form and flew down to enter the window. Landing on the floor, she became human, shivering from the cold.

Ronan glanced towards the door. "What are you doing here, kitten? Brigitte hasn't long since left."

"I know. What are the two of you planning?"

Ronan took the blanket off the rumpled bed and

draped it around her shoulders. "You're shivering. Are you trying to get sick?"

"Don't change the subject. What are the two of you planning?"

"Our plans haven't changed."

"Then what do you want with Keeley. Your granddaughter." She smiled when Ronan stilled. "You didn't know."

"Brigitte obviously doesn't tell me everything."

"What does she tell you and what do you want with Keeley? Talk to me, Ronan. I'm guessing you will want me to rescue you, eventually."

"Who says I'll need you to rescue me, kitten?" His predatory smile formed. "Brigitte is a queen without a king to help and support her in her many plans."

Amber laughed. "Something tells me she's not that much of a fool to fall for a line like that."

"We have many shared memories and experiences. I've been reminding her of them."

All the things she'd learned about Brigitte had her slowly shaking her head. "I've got a feeling she's nothing like the person you once knew."

"No, she's a lot more interesting these days."

Fear raced through Amber. There was no way she'd let Ronan make a permanent alliance with Brigitte. Struggling to hold the blanket around herself, she pointed a finger at him. "You will not do anything stupid. That woman must die." She wasn't about to let her live in the same world as those she loved. Kade was Gold and all Brigitte seemed interested in was the heart of a Gold. Who knew what she might do. Or who she might go after.

Ronan captured her hand, keeping the blanket from slipping with his other hand. "What do you know, kitten?"

"She's evil."

"That has been said of me more than once."

"She would kill her own kids for selfish reasons."

"Many dragons kill their offspring when they fail them or bring dishonour to their clan."

She met Ronan's gaze, trying to discover what he was thinking. All she could see in his gold eyes was her image reflected back at her. "Are you planning to ally yourself with her?"

"Why is this so important to you, kitten?"

"Because she can't be trusted. She'd break a promise without hesitation. You could never count on her to keep her word."

"What have you been told?"

"Do you trust me, Ronan?"

"With my life, Amber."

Shock raced through her.

Ronan chuckled. "Didn't expect that, now did you?"

Not in the least, but she kept that thought to herself. "Then trust me on this. That woman makes alarm bells ring every time I look at her. She's dangerous. Not because of her capabilities, but because of what she might do. On a whim. Because it suits her. And because she doesn't care about anyone other than herself. Do not make any deals with her that will ally the two of you. I won't have her in your life."

"If you were a dragon, I'd think you were being possessive."

"I am, but not of you. Are you not mine, Ronan?" She flung his own words back at him, words he'd asked her previously.

"You already know the answer to that, kitten."

She mimicked his predatory smile. "Then you will listen when I say that I will end her life before I allow her in our lives and near those who are mine. All those who are mine."

"This is about Kade and Crystal."

"Isn't it always?"

He studied her for a moment. "Not always, kitten. Not always."

She was tempted to ask him what he meant with

how softly he said the words, but she knew him well enough to know he wouldn't answer her. "I can break the magic of the bracelet."

Again Ronan stilled.

She grinned. "Surprised again, Ronan?"

"Apparently you're full of surprises today, kitten." He let go of her hand, first clamping it over the blanket so she could hold it in place. He turned away from her, the chain rattling as he did so. "Would she know?"

"I don't know."

"Then we leave it for now." He faced her again. "Until she's laid an egg, I will not have her realise I'm plotting against her."

Relief rushed through her at his words. "Okay."

"What else have you learned?"

She briefly told him what had happened since she'd last spoken to him, finishing with needing to talk to Keeley.

"Extend an invitation to her to visit me in our world," Ronan said.

"Why?"

"Have you considered that I might wish to get to know my granddaughter?"

"Not at all. Now what are you planning, Ronan?"

"The world will know that I have more than one

Gold offspring. That there have been several as well as grandchildren."

She slowly shook her head. "Of course you'd want that."

"It's all about power, kitten. Surely you know that by now. Only the strongest survive."

She started to take a step away from him when another idea occurred to her. "Where would Brigitte keep her bracelets? She's meant to have thousands of them. So where would she keep them?"

"What are you planning?"

She grinned at the way he mocked her earlier words. "You don't think you're the only one who can plot and plan, do you?"

"Well?"

She glanced at the metal band around his wrist. "It doesn't have to be her bracelet as long as it does the same job."

"You thinking of binding me to you?"

Hearing the warning in his tone, she kept her voice light. "I have enough headaches without you being powerless and needing to be taken care of."

"You think me powerless like this?"

Chapter Fourteen

Again Amber heard the warning in Ronan's tone. Pushing the blanket aside enough to reach past it, she lightly patted his cheek. "Don't worry, Ronan, it's not like it'll last." For a second she almost thought she could mentally reach him.

He grabbed her by the wrist. "Do you think me powerless?"

She stepped forward rather than break away from his grip, meeting his gaze. "With the speed at which you hatch plots, I doubt you'd ever be powerless. Physical limitations or weaknesses don't mean being without power."

He continued to grip her wrist, his gaze meeting hers. "Don't you forget that, kitten."

"There's one other thing I'm not about to forget."

"And what is that?"

"You owe me. If you hadn't dragged me away half

prepared, then we wouldn't be in this predicament. I could have returned home for reinforcements."

"It's a good thing I did drag you away half prepared."

She stared at him, playing the words over in her mind several times. They made as little sense to her as they had the first time. "What is that supposed to mean? How can it be good that we're stuck here?"

Ronan's predatory smile formed. "There's a chance I'll end up with a Gold offspring out of this."

"Poor kid."

Ronan chuckled. "Do you really think that? What about Rian? I raised the boy and you seem rather fond of him."

"Amber," Treon thought to her.

"What?"

"About fifty hybrids approach the castle, none of them hidden. Are you unharmed?"

At his warning, she searched the area further afield, easily finding them. None of them had hunters riding them. *"I'm unharmed."*

"Have you spoken to Keeley yet?" Treon asked.

"What is going on?" Ronan demanded.

Amber held up a hand, answering Treon first. *"No. Shortly though. I'll let you know when I see her."*

"Thank you."

"Amber." Once again there was a warning note in Ronan's voice.

She lowered her hand. "Fifty hybrids approach."

"Probably the ones she sent for since there's been unrest at Cliffview."

"You didn't think to tell me that when I was telling you about Gunsa?"

"Don't go getting yourself killed, kitten."

"Then don't go keeping information from me. I gave her my word I'd help her get her children back."

"What the hybrids do isn't your problem."

She started to argue his comment, closing her mouth instead. She searched the area again. The hybrids had nearly reached the castle. "I need to see Keeley before I leave."

"Don't go doing anything stupid," Ronan warned.

Amber grinned at him. "You worried you might end up stuck here if something happened to me?"

"No. That would never happen."

Her grin faded. He was probably right. If anyone could turn a situation to his advantage, it was Ronan. "I'll be back as soon as possible." After she found where Brigitte stored the bracelets. She held out the blanket, shivering at the cool air. Even inside the temperature wasn't as warm as she liked it.

Ronan took the blanket. "Keeley is in the dungeon.

It'll be easiest to enter from outside. About half a metre of the cells are above ground and they have barred windows that let in the light. And the cold."

"Thank you." She walked to the window, sensing that Ronan remained where he was. Becoming a goshawk, she dived towards the ground, keeping close to the walls to hopefully avoid the notice of the couple of hybrids that were on this side of the castle. She mentally searched the area, finding that Keeley was alone. She didn't know if Brigitte had already visited her or if she'd been distracted from her plans by the arrival of the hybrids. Reaching the barred window, Amber perched on it and squeezed between the bars, flying down to land beside Keeley who was sitting in front of a wall, hand outstretched.

Keeley lowered her hand, sighing as she looked up at Amber who became human. "He was so close."

Amber frowned. "What?"

Keeley nodded towards the wall. "The rat. I'd nearly convinced him to come to me."

Amber stared at the wall, noticing a whiskered nose poke out of a crack between two of the roughly hewn rocks, drawing back immediately. "A rat."

Keeley grinned. "I thought it was better to concentrate on encouraging him to come to me than to think on ways to find a weapon and use it on

Brigitte. It's long past time she died, but I dread to think what it would do to Mum."

Amber debated not passing along the message from Morgane.

Keeley rose to her feet. "Is something wrong?"

Amber took a deep breath before she passed along the message, wondering if she'd done the right thing.

"That bothers you," Keeley said.

Amber shrugged. She didn't know any of them well enough to know how they'd react if Keeley was the one to take Brigitte out. Not that she wanted to be the one either. She tried not to think about the hybrids. "Your brother is worried about you."

"Did he send a message too?"

"He wants me to let him know when I'm with you."

Keeley smiled. "How did you manage to come without any of them?" Her smile faded. "I keep expecting Mum to come charging in here leaving destruction in her wake as she tries to save me."

"She probably realises that would only get the two of you killed."

"I'm surprised Brigitte hasn't already killed me. Your companion talked her into keeping me alive for a few days as he wanted to learn about the mix of hunters and dragons and what we're capable of. I don't think he knows who I am and I wasn't about to tell him. There's something about him I can't read. Maybe you know. Is he good or bad?"

She thought about the many things she'd learned about Ronan. "Neither. But he does have a strong code he lives by. His word is his law and his life. You can trust him to do what he promises."

"The problem is that he sidestepped around the questions Brigitte asked him and the plans she wanted to involve him in. He gave no real answers or any promises. How can a person like that be trusted?"

Amber found herself mimicking Ronan's predatory smile. "Because when you do get a promise out of him you can trust he'll follow through on it."

Keeley's gaze was drawn to Amber's lips. "You're close to him."

Amber laughed. "I don't think anyone is close to Ronan."

"Maybe not, but I think you are."

Amber wasn't sure what she thought about that. "You're Gold."

Keeley frowned. "I don't understand what that has to do with our conversation."

"Nothing." Amber shrugged. "I get distracted sometimes." Although she didn't get as distracted as much as she once did. "Would you be willing to hold a Pliethin and unlock your abilities?"

"I'm only half a dragon."

Amber thought of her cousin, Shylah. "That makes no difference. You're Gold. You could learn how to travel through the Void."

Keeley held up her arm, the metal band at eye height. "What about this?"

"I can remove it, but not yet. I don't want to risk Brigitte discovering you've had a visitor. What I really need to do is find out where she keeps them."

"That's easy. They're down here in a cell guarded by eight hybrids. Brigitte had them open the door so she could put a bracelet on me." Keeley gestured to the left. "Four cells that way."

Amber stared at Keeley. Surely it couldn't be that easy to find them. "Are you sure?"

Keeley nodded. "There were thousands of them in open crates."

"I need to get one and see if anyone can get it to work or if only Brigitte can."

"The cell has a barred window like this one."

"I need to have a look." Amber took a step towards the window.

"What about Treon? Did you tell him you're with me yet?"

Amber smiled wryly. "Sorry. I forgot." She mentally reached for Treon. *"I'm with your sister."*

"Is she unharmed?"

Amber studied the half dragon. There were a few bruises, but apart from that, she seemed fine. *"Yeah, she's okay."*

"Tell her we'll get her out of there," Treon said.

Amber passed along the message.

"Tell Treon that I won't have any of them risk their lives for me. I'd rather end it than know I was the cause of their death."

Amber hesitated.

"You're not going to tell him, are you?" Keeley asked.

Sighing, she passed along the message.

"If she ends things, then so will I. You tell her that," Treon warned.

"Bloody dragons," Amber muttered.

"What did he say?" Keeley asked.

Amber repeated his warning.

Keeley laughed. "That sounds so much like him. I wish I could talk to him."

Thinking of the earlier sensation of when she'd briefly touched Ronan's cheek, Amber stepped forward. "Maybe you can." She placed her hand against Keeley's cheek, surprised at how warm she was.

"Your hand is cold."

Amber ignored Treon asking her what was wrong and why she was silent. She concentrated on Keeley, trying to reach her. For a second she did, connecting the siblings.

Treon fell silent for a moment. *"That was Keeley. Can you do that again?"*

Amber started to lower her hand. *"Sorry. I don't think I can make it last any longer than that."*

Keeley grabbed her hand, pressing it against her skin. "Can you try again? I really want to talk to him. You can't imagine how much I've missed my family. I wouldn't have thought it possible. It hasn't been a day."

She saw the fear in Keeley's eyes and heard the words she didn't speak. The ones of death and wanting to speak a few last words to her family. "Brigitte isn't going to kill you." She kept her hand against Keeley's cheek. "We'll get you out of here before that can happen." There were so many things that needed to be done. So many people that needed to be saved. She tried not to think of them, but they filled her mind anyway. Ronan, Gunsa's children, Keeley. She dreaded to think how many more there'd be considering how little time she'd been in this world.

"You're hurting?"

Amber started to deny it, nodding instead. "Not physically."

"This is why I trust you."

"What?" Amber frowned. "That doesn't make any sense."

Keeley laughed softly. "Your pain. You don't know us, but you're willing to risk your life for me and it pains you that you might not be able to save me."

"You're not the only one." Once more she ignored Treon's demands to know what was going on, trying instead to connect the two siblings.

"Who else is in danger?" Keeley asked.

Amber grinned when she mentally reached Keeley, this time for several seconds, connecting the two siblings again. She felt the flow of emotions between them. It reminded her of her family. Both those who were blood related and those she'd made a part of her family. She longed for home.

"Thank you." Keeley's words echoed those of her brother and she wrapped her arms around Amber. "Thank you so much."

Chapter Fifteen

Amber returned Keely's hug before stepping away, wishing she could remain against the warmth of Keeley's body rather than face the cold. Somehow she managed to prevent a smile, doubting the hunter-dragon would appreciate being likened to a hot water bottle. "I'll return as soon as I can." Turning into a goshawk she again slipped between the bars, searching the area to her left. There were two warriors hidden from her. A hybrid and a hunter. From where they stood she assumed they guarded the bracelets. She reached for Treon. *"Can you help me?"*

"Name it."

"I need to get a bracelet from where Brigitte keeps them and she has two guards outside the window."

"Do you want me to kill them?"

"No. That shouldn't be necessary. They aren't standing

right against the wall so I'm hoping I can sneak in behind them if you can get me close enough."

"Tell me where you are."

"Thank you." She directed him to where she was, landing on his back as he came close.

"Thank you for helping me contact my sister."

"We'll have her out of there soon." Amber directed him to where she needed to go, getting him to stay close to the castle wall. When they reached the window, she flew the short distance to the ledge, squeezing through the bars. She tracked the movements of the two warriors as she grabbed one of the bracelets in her claws, flying back to the window ledge. She placed the bracelet on it so she could slip through the bars. The two warriors remained where they were. It was a pity she couldn't tell which direction they were looking in. Taking a deep breath, she picked up the bracelet, drawing it between the bars before flying the short distance to Treon's back. *"Get us out of here. Fly straight up until you're well above them."* She struggled to stay on his back, but remained silent. They needed to get away from here. She had no idea what might happen if she was caught trying to steal a bracelet, but doubted it'd be anything good.

When they were well above the castle, she checked on the warriors. They hadn't moved. *"Land as soon as we're well away from the castle. We need to see how this bracelet works."*

"We should return to my family and let them know Keeley is well," Treon said.

"We don't have time." She briefly told him what she'd learned, including information about the coming attack on Cliffview.

Treon landed on a slope well away from the castle, waiting until she was off his back before he shapeshifted. "You plan to stop her."

Amber became human, holding the bracelet out to him. "If we take out the hybrids currently guarding the village and move everyone out before morning we won't have to face a force we can't beat."

"We don't know how many hybrids are at the village." Treon snapped the bracelet shut on his wrist, holding his arm out to her.

Like the previous time, she whispered Kade's name against the metal band.

"What word did you use?"

She looked up at him, her gaze clashing with his. He was a dragon. She doubted telling him she'd used the name of another male to bind him would sit well. His expression changed slightly and she tried to figure out what it meant. But she didn't know him well enough.

He raised the bracelet to his lips, whispering against it. Lowering his arm, he opened the bracelet.

This time she recognised his expression and grinned, shrugging in response.

"You used the name of your lover to bind me?"

She laughed. "Apparently."

He held the bracelet out to her.

She shook her head. "You try."

He put the bracelet back on and snapped it shut, whispering against it. "The bracelet works no matter who puts it on me."

"Good." This time she took it when he held it out to her. "We need a Pliethin. Do you think one of the children who've caught one would part with it?"

"What do you need it for?"

"Keeley."

"She's happy to use one even though we don't know what it might do to the hunter in her?"

"She didn't decline." Amber kept to herself that Keeley also hadn't agreed.

"How many do you need?"

Amber shrugged. "Do you think your aunt would be interested? And what about you? Did you want to try it?"

"I don't want to risk losing my hunter abilities."

She didn't blame him. Becoming invisible was handy at times. "Okay. Can you get two?"

"Yeah." He shapeshifted. *"Ready to go?"*

Amber put the bracelet on her wrist, not sure if it'd shapeshift with her, but willing to try rather than have to carry it. She changed into a panther, not wanting to risk that it might break a wing if she turned into a goshawk and it didn't shift with her. She looked at each limb. There was no bracelet. When it wasn't activated, it shifted with the wearer. Becoming human, she couldn't resist grinning as she clambered onto Treon's back.

"What was that for?"

She explained it to him.

"That is useful."

Amber nodded. Now she just needed a second bracelet for Ronan and to get them to both of Brigitte's prisoners.

Night had long since fallen by the time Treon landed beside a lake, the light of the moon reflected on its surface. He shapeshifted once Amber was on the ground. "I won't be long. You'll be safe here."

She took a step towards him, automatically searching the area. "You're going to leave me in a forest?" Nearby were numerous people, around her only small forest animals.

"I can't take you into my village. It'd take too long to go through all the formalities. We don't have time for that."

She wanted to protest. Instead, she drew in a deep breath, reminding herself that she was a warrior. Yet at times she didn't feel like one. Especially now when she was stuck in a strange world and about to be left alone in a forest with unknown dangers.

"I trusted you to put the bracelet on me." Treon glanced at the metal band on Amber's wrist.

"I'll wait here for you." She somehow managed not to tell him to hurry.

He studied her a moment longer before he inclined his head and strode towards the village.

Amber watched him go, the entire time scanning the area for danger. Nothing changed. Everything was still the same when he returned what felt like hours later, but Amber assumed was probably only half an hour. A woman walked at his side. When they drew near, her similarities to Morgane had her pretty certain she knew who was with him.

Treon stopped in front of Amber. "My sister. Ninian."

The woman looked Amber up and down. "You are the one who'll save our sister?"

Amber didn't know if she should feel offended at the tone of Ninian's voice. "That's the plan."

"How much experience have you had at this?"

"Ninian–"

Amber interrupted Treon. "It's okay. I'd want to know who was to rescue those I loved too." Although she didn't know if she could stay back if it was one of her people imprisoned.

"I want to help," Ninian stated.

"Nin–"

Ninian spun to face her brother, interrupting him. "She's my sister too."

Amber recognised the fierce tone. "We need warriors to rescue the people of Cliffview."

"How will that help my sister?" Ninian demanded.

"It will weaken Brigitte. At the moment she's too strong to face head on." Amber wished Ronan was here. With his centuries of experience he'd be able to come up with an unbeatable plan. There were so many things that needed to be done. She didn't know if she was up to the task.

"All I care about is keeping my family safe," Ninian stated.

"As long as Brigitte lives, your family is in danger," Amber warned.

Ninian held her gaze for a moment before

inclining her head. "I've said for years that she must die. But none are more powerful than her. Unless it's the savages. They have some of the fiercest fighters."

"The enemy of my enemy-"

Treon interrupted Amber. "They have no allies. They fight amongst themselves. Unless Brigitte attacked them, they wouldn't worry about her due to how far she lives from them."

Amber started to ask him more, shaking her head instead. "We don't have time for any of this. I have to get a Pliethin to Keeley and change her bracelet. Did you get any Pliethins?"

Ninian slipped off a small leather backpack Amber hadn't noticed before. "Here." She held it out to Amber.

Taking it, Amber looked inside. Two jars containing Pliethins were nestled amongst soft cloths. The jars were so small that the Pliethins filled them. "Thanks." She started to take out one of the jars.

Ninian rested a hand on hers, preventing her. "The backpack is made of dragon-leather. It'll shift with you."

Amber slipped the backpack into place. "Thanks."

"I still wish to come with you," Ninian said.

"Can you take a message to your family?" Amber asked.

"Are you trying to keep me out of the way?" Ninian demanded.

Amber laughed. "No. Although I'll have to keep that technique in mind next time I do want to keep someone out of the way. I need someone to tell your family what's going on. I would ask Treon, but he can make me invisible so I need him to help me reach Keeley."

"What do you want me to tell them?"

"About the attack on Cliffview. We need to get everyone out of the village before that happens. Also, do you know of any other dragons who can help carry them to safety?" Amber asked.

"I'll see who's willing to help." Ninian turned to Treon. "Tell Keeley to play it safe. We want her to come home."

"Is that something I have to worry about?" Amber asked.

Treon shrugged. "Sometimes. She's the most patient of all of us, but when her patience wears out, she tends to do crazy things in an effort to get things done."

Amber managed not to groan at the news. As if she needed any other problems. "Okay. Let's get moving. We're running out of time."

Treon rested a hand on his sister's shoulder. "We'll meet in the forest south of Cliffview."

Ninian nodded, remaining where she was as the two of them flew towards Brigitte's castle.

Amber kept track of her as they left, strengthening her ties to the hunter-dragon. She couldn't help wondering what Ronan would think of all his grandchildren. He couldn't fault their strength of character, but he might not appreciate the way they were willing to risk themselves for each other.

It was after midnight, according to Treon, when they reached Brigitte's castle. Amber tried to stifle a yawn, but it escaped anyway.

"Are you going to last long enough to get all of this done?"

Amber nodded, searching out the cat she'd noticed yesterday. It was curled up towards the back of the castle on the ground floor, no one else nearby. "Yeah. Can you take me around to the other side of the building?"

"What is around there?" He flew around the castle, avoiding the hybrids that Amber mentioned.

She didn't know if she should tell him. Very few knew all the secrets of creating Dragon Mages.

"Aren't we here to help my sister?"

"Yes." When they reached the other side of the

castle, she became a goshawk, flying towards a window. *"Wait here."* She again searched the area. It was still clear. She landed in front of the cat, which was curled up by the fireplace, only glowing coals remaining. When it opened its eyes, Amber hurriedly became human, not wanting to risk becoming its meal. She ran her hand across its sleek, black fur. Some of it clung to her hand. She tucked the loose bits of fur into the waistband of her trousers so they were pressed against her skin.

The cat purred, closing its eyes again.

"Thank you." She whispered the words, running her hand along the cat's back once more before rising to her feet. She had no idea if it would work or how good a plan it was. But she needed a less obvious animal and hopefully she was about to give a Gold a Pliethin.

Chapter Sixteen

Becoming a goshawk, Amber flew back out the window to Treon, landing on his back.

"What were you doing in there?" Treon asked.

"Not much. Ready to take me to your sister now?"

"Let me know where the warriors are."

She directed him to Keeley's window, glad there were no warriors posted outside it like there were for the cell that contained the bracelets. She slipped through the bars, flying inside to land in front of Keeley, glad of her ability to see in limited light. She shapeshifted when Keeley sat up, having been curled up on the floor, wrapped in a thin blanket.

"Have you come to take me out of here? It's so cold when I can't keep my body temperature up as much as it normally is."

Amber was tempted to point out that Keeley's temperature was far warmer than her own. She unsnapped the bracelet. "Ready to exchange that one for one you control?"

Keeley rose to her feet, letting the blanket fall to the floor. "Yes. You can't imagine how difficult it is not being able to use abilities that have been such a big part of my life."

She had a good idea of how easy it was to rely on them and how hard it was not to automatically use them. "Before you wear this bracelet, would you like to try using a Pliethin?" She slipped the backpack off her shoulders, drawing out one of the jars. It had been a good thing Ninian had put them in a dragon-leather backpack or she had no idea how she would have been able to bring them into the cell.

Keeley stared at the jar. "Will it hurt?"

"I don't know. I've only ever experienced it as a Dragon Mage. But I have held one twice."

Keeley nodded, straightening her shoulders. "One of us needs to try it and see what it can do for us. Or to us."

Amber set the jar, bracelet and backpack on the floor. "I'll remove that first." She nodded towards the metal band on Keeley's wrist.

Keeley held out her hand, smiling. "Thank you."

"You might not say that after I'm finished." Amber

wrapped a hand around the metal band, forcing fireballs into it.

Keeley laughed softly. "At least it's warming."

The bracelet dropped to the floor and Amber winced at the sound, wishing she'd wrapped both hands around it, or turned it so the opening was beneath her palm. She mentally searched the area around them. The only warriors were those guarding the door and window of the cell with the bracelets. None of them moved.

Keeley threw her arms around Amber, holding her tightly. "Getting rid of that feels amazing. I feel like myself again." She grinned. "And I can talk to Treon."

Amber returned the hug before pulling away. "I need some of your blood." She wasn't about to take the chance that hunter-dragon blood was different to plain dragon blood. She'd do everything possible to make the Pliethin work for her. She needed every advantage possible if she was going to take Brigitte down with how little she had at her disposal. She couldn't help thinking about Temolae Keep. Normally she had a castle of warriors when she needed them.

"An exchange then," Keeley offered.

Amber frowned, the words not making sense. "Exchange?"

"Yes. My blood in exchange for yours. If you can follow my signature then I should be able to follow yours."

"I don't need your blood to follow your signature. I can easily track down most of your family."

Keeley tilted her head slightly. "That isn't a threat? Your body language and tone says it's not, yet normally such words would be a threat."

"No, it's not a threat. I'm the one who tracked you down. I'm also the one who helped Ronan track down Brigitte."

"That is a very powerful ability."

Amber didn't bother mentioning that it didn't always work if she hadn't strengthened the tie and a person was good at hiding themselves. Like Fredrick. Next time he came after her, she'd be prepared and make sure she'd be able to find him no matter where he went. She drew one of her daggers, pricking her skin before holding the dagger out to Keeley.

"You do understand that this means you won't be able to hide from me should I ever go looking for you." Keeley took the dagger.

Amber grinned. "There is more than this world." She took back the dagger once Keeley was finished with it, sheathing it before offering her hand to the hunter-dragon.

Keeley held out her hand. "I won't use the offering against you."

Amber couldn't bring herself to offer the same. "If you don't come after me or mine then I have no reason to come after you or yours."

Keeley inclined her head before lowering it and pressing her lips to the blood on Amber's hand she held.

Amber did the same, breathing in sharply as the blood entered her system. It felt different to dragon blood. Sharper. Like the world had more edges and was brighter. She raised her head to stare at Keeley, keeping hold of her hand. "Are you ready for the Pliethin?"

"Yes."

"I'll hold it for a moment before giving it to you. Whatever you do, you mustn't let it go until the light fades. You also need to become a dragon after you take the Pliethin."

"I understand."

Amber let go of Keeley's hand and picked up the glass jar, unscrewing the lid. She grabbed hold of the Pliethin as it tried to escape, feeling the tingling of it against her hand. "Don't struggle. You can return to your own world soon." She had no idea where its world was, but maybe one day she'd track one back to where it came from.

Keeley took the Pliethin when Amber held it out to her. The moment her hands touched the Pliethin, a rat raced down her arm from where it had been hidden amongst her hair, squealing as it raced across their joined hands before dropping onto the floor and scurrying back to the crack between the stones.

Amber nearly let go of the Pliethin before Keeley had a proper hold of it, startled by the rat. She stepped back once the hunter-dragon had the Pliethin, holding back the demands she wanted to make. What had Keeley been doing with the rat? Why hadn't she set it down before taking the Pliethin? And why hadn't it scurried away when she'd stood up? The questions would have to wait. She couldn't distract Keeley.

The hunter-dragon shapeshifted, continuing to hold the Pliethin, her head thrown back as her patchwork of silver and gold scales were bathed in the glow of the creature. When the Pliethin became a grey, shapeless ball, she became human, dropping to the floor, her head lowered. "Should I feel so drained?"

Amber took the Pliethin from her, thanking it

before she opened her hands and let it fade from the world. "Yeah. It won't take you too long to recover." She handed the bracelet to Keeley. "Don't activate it straight away. I don't know how it will affect your Gold abilities if you do."

"Thank you." Keeley took the bracelet then struggled to rise to her feet.

Amber picked up the blanket and draped it over her shoulders. "Rest." She glanced towards where the rat had disappeared. "Why did you have the rat with you?"

Keeley wrapped the blanket around her shoulders. "He was cold. I don't think he would have approached me otherwise. Why? Is it a problem?"

Amber shook her head, keeping her thoughts to herself. She really hoped it didn't alter what she'd tried to do. "I need to go. We have other things to do before dawn." She picked up the backpack and returned the jar and broken bracelet to it before slipping the backpack into place.

Again Keeley tried to get to her feet.

Amber pressed lightly on her shoulder. "Rest. You can't slip through the bars. When you do have the opportunity to escape, do. They won't be expecting you to turn into a dragon. We've taken back your parents' castle."

"What else do you have to do?" Keeley remained on the floor, looking up at Amber.

She wasn't about to tell the hunter-dragon everything. Who knew what she might attempt if she learned they were to attack Cliffview. "I need to replace Ronan's bracelet with one he can control." She gestured towards the bracelet Keeley had set on the floor beside herself. "Make sure you put that on and activate it before anyone comes into the cell."

"I will." Keeley smiled up at Amber. "You can't imagine how grateful I am for all you've done for us. I knew you could be trusted the moment I saw you."

She mentally debated with herself about warning Keeley. A sigh escaped. "Sometimes I'm bound to side with my ally."

"My grandfather."

"I don't think that will help you with him. He might not be as bad as Brigitte, but there isn't much he won't do to survive."

"Yet you're his ally."

A wry smile formed as Amber thought of how that had come about. "Yeah. I don't think it was meant to be as permanent as it is." She took a step towards the window, the chill in the air making her want to be anything other than human. "Ninian is worried you'll take unnecessary risks. Don't. Your family need you alive for all that's coming."

"What is coming?"

Amber stopped by the window, looking over her shoulder at Keeley who had the blanket wrapped around her body. She looked young and innocent considering the years she'd lived from the various comments she'd heard. "War."

"You can't know that."

She knew Ronan and he wasn't about to give up his offspring if it was Gold. Nor would he allow Brigitte to get away with imprisoning him. "Yeah, I can." Becoming a goshawk, she landed on the ledge and slipped outside, mentally reaching for Treon to let him know she needed to make another visit to the cell containing the bracelets. She thought of her own bracelets. The ones containing her power and the ones needing to be filled. When war came, they wouldn't be enough.

"Thank you for what you did for Keeley," Treon said. She landed on his back. *"She isn't safe yet."*

"She might not be, but now she has a chance. She's a fierce warrior and capable of holding her own against most enemies. What you've done will allow her to fight."

"I'm hoping what I've done will allow her to flee so she can regroup with us and we can fight from a stronger

position." She directed Treon to the window, having him stay close to the wall since there were still two warriors guarding Brigitte's possessions from outside. They were different to the earlier ones.

Reaching the window, she landed on the ledge and slipped inside, becoming human once she landed on the floor. She shoved a bracelet in the backpack, hesitating before she shoved a second one in. Her gaze was drawn to each of the crates. Something had to be done about them. They couldn't allow Brigitte to continue to use them. Although getting rid of these wouldn't matter if Brigitte still had the means to make more.

Amber stilled. They had to get rid of the hunter. Once again she was about to plot the death of someone. Reminding herself of all the hunter had been a part of, she slipped the backpack into place before becoming a goshawk. It took her a second to make the shift, a confusion of animals at her call. Again she found herself holding still as she drank in the knowledge of what she'd done. How was she going to sort through four animals when she wanted to shapeshift? Three had seemed like a lot to cope with. Four seemed impossible.

"*Is something wrong?*" Treon thought to Amber.

"*I'll be out in a second.*" Pushing her concerns away,

she flew up to the window ledge and slipped through the bars, checking the warriors as she did so. They hadn't moved. She had no idea how they stayed in place when it was so cold, the temperature feeling like it had dropped yet another couple of degrees. She was definitely taking a holiday somewhere tropical when she was finally able to leave this world.

Treon flew upwards the moment Amber landed on his back, following her directions to Ronan's window. He hovered outside. *"Are you going in?"*

She wasn't sure if she should tell him Brigitte was in the bed with Ronan. How good was her hearing? And would Brigitte suspect anything if Amber used the house cat form? She supposed there was only one way to find out. *"Fly upwards and stay on the roof until I call you. There's no one up there."* She landed on the window ledge, trying to figure out how to become a cat as she dropped to the floor. Nothing happened. She flew low across the floor, landing under the bed as she tried to sort through all the animals. Even her two she could normally change into felt unfamiliar. What had she done? This was meant to help. After the amount of time she'd been shapeshifting she hadn't expected it to become so difficult to access her usual animals. Especially not when it was only a cat, not some wild animal.

Chapter Seventeen

Above Amber one of them moved in the bed, only Brigitte in dragon form. She stilled, worried she'd woken someone. Their breathing remained even and neither of them moved again. After another minute Amber again tried to become a cat. Somehow she shifted into a rat. Not at all what she'd wanted. Another attempt had her becoming a human. She barely suppressed a frustrated growl. Once more she tried, almost cheering when she became a cat, her black fur matching that of the cat she'd taken the fur from. Creeping out from under the bed, she mentally searched the room again. Only Ronan and Brigitte were here and both were either asleep or pretending to be.

She jumped lightly onto the bed, remaining at the edge until she was certain neither of them moved. Taking several steps forward, she again searched the area. Nothing had changed. Placing a paw against Ronan, she tried to reach him, managing for long enough to sense his amusement and hear him think the word 'kitten'. Before she could do anything else Brigitte shapeshifted and sat up.

"Throw that mangy cat out of the bed. It belongs downstairs."

"I'd offer to take it down there for you, but I'm rather attached to this bed," Ronan said dryly.

Brigitte laughed softly, leaning over Ronan. "Are you complaining, Ro?"

Amber felt him tense at the nickname, the action so slight and fleeting she would have missed it if she hadn't been at his side.

"Why would I complain at having you at my beck and call?" Ronan asked mildly.

Brigitte sat up, moving away from him. "I am not at your beck and call."

"Aren't you? That's not what I heard a few hours ago." Ronan's lips curved into his predatory smile as he reached for her. "Shall we find out?"

Glaring at him, Brigitte left the bed, taking a blanket with her and wrapping it around her body. "You and the mangy cat can spend the night elsewhere."

Amber sensed warriors headed towards the

bedroom. She dug her claws into Ronan's arm to warn him he might be going too far.

Ronan patted her on the head.

She glared up at him, quickly looking away when warriors dragged him from the bed and Brigitte threw his trousers at him before he was dragged from the room, one of the warriors having unlocked the chain.

Brigitte advanced on Amber. "You too. Get out of here and catch rodents."

Amber swiped at Brigitte on the way past, scurrying out of the way of the kick aimed at her. She hissed at the dragon as she scurried after Ronan, relieved to find the warriors had allowed him to pull on his trousers. When he was shoved inside a cell, she slipped past the warriors as they left, barely getting inside before they slammed the door shut. She waited until they were no longer in the area before she became human, the only form it was easy for her to take.

"What have you been up to, kitten?" He stressed the last word.

She looked him up and down, his shirt and boots missing. "Not as much as you, apparently."

Ronan chuckled. "I hope you have a good reason for disturbing me since I'm now in for a cold night and I'm going to assume you haven't changed your mind about throwing Kade aside for me."

She slipped off the backpack, leaving it on the floor before she wrapped her hands around his wrist. "Swapping out your bracelet for one you can control."

"And you said you haven't been as busy as me. Are you taking to lying to me now, kitten?"

She forced fireballs into the bracelet, catching it before it could fall to the floor. "As if."

"I don't have Golds watching your every move here."

She crouched in front of the backpack and took out one of the bracelets. "I'm not about to go against you, Ronan. Haven't we already settled that?" He pulled away from her when she tried to put the bracelet on him. "What now?"

"Why is there a Pliethin in your backpack and what else have you been up to?"

Amber held the bracelet out to Ronan. "Here. You put it on then." Once he'd taken it, she put the broken one in the backpack, which she then slipped back into place.

"Well?" Ronan snapped the bracelet around his wrist.

Amber sighed. She didn't have time to go over

everything. Not if she wanted to get to Cliffview before the hybrids attacked.

"What are you keeping from me?"

"Nothing. I just don't have time for this. I have somewhere to be before dawn."

"You're going to save Cliffview."

"Did you really think I'd let them be slaughtered? It'll also weaken Brigitte's position." She gestured towards the bracelet he now wore. "Not that it matters anymore. You'll be able to get away from here when it suits you."

Ronan grabbed her by the shoulders, drawing her close, his gaze meeting hers. "You will not get yourself killed over people you don't know. Stop collecting the lame and useless."

"Haven't I also collected you?" She forced a smile to her lips, ignoring the urge to pull away from his grip.

"With the amount you collect you have to get lucky sometimes."

Amber's smile became less forced. "I will tell you everything. Just not now. I have to go, Ronan."

"Then why did you bother to see me if you're so lacking in time?"

"Because I couldn't leave you at Brigitte's mercy when she has none. Now let me go, Ronan. I have people to save, a war to plan and a hunter to track down."

"War? What have you got us into?" Ronan demanded.

"Me? Absolutely nothing. I'm preparing for the plans you're going to make. Or are you going to let Brigitte keep your offspring if it's Gold?"

Ronan studied her a moment before letting her go. "I will be involved in any plans made on my behalf."

"Like you always involve me in plans you make on my behalf?" She took a step back from him and closer to the window.

Ronan pointed a warning finger at her. "Don't try me, kitten."

Amber again smiled at him, this time mimicking his predatory one. "I wouldn't dream of it." She tried twice before she managed to become a goshawk, relieved that Ronan wouldn't have realised her dilemma. She mentally reached for Treon, directing him to where she was, not answering Ronan when he warned her she better return to him after she finished at Cliffview.

Treon swooped down in front of her, flying upwards as soon as she landed on his back, circling around to head towards Cliffview. *"Were you able to help your companion?"*

She became human, clinging to his back as she settled into place, grinning at Treon's question. "I think he's beyond help." She sensed Treon's answering humour, her smile fading as the cold settled into her bones. The dragon-leather helped, but nowhere near enough. She couldn't wait to spend a few weeks on a tropical beach. Just her and Kade stretched out on the warm sand and soaking in the sun. She could almost feel his arms wrapped around her, the fine grains of sand pressed against her skin. Closing her eyes, she breathed out heavily. She would see him again soon. Ronan would have to accept disappointment. She wasn't about to stay here for a week. She wanted to go home.

Their journey was silent and Amber figured out where they were to meet up long before they reached it. Many of those she'd strengthened ties with waited there for them, including her prisoners. She was relieved to find them amongst the group. They'd make it easier to get everyone out of Cliffview.

They arrived at the clearing in the forest south of Cliffview to catch the end of an argument, the results being that Gunsa and the other three hunters would lead two people into the village with the dead bracelets on so they could take out two of the hybrids before they realised what was going on. Gunsa wanted to sneak as many of her people as they could out first. In the end, it was agreed that two of the hunters would sneak out the people on the outskirts of the village while Gunsa and the other hunter took supposed captives into the villages.

Amber dismounted. "I have two broken bracelets and one that hasn't been broken." She took the Pliethin, which was in a jar, out of the backpack. "I also have this for Caral."

"I don't know if I want to use it. How do we know it'll work the same in this world as in the world dragons come from?" Caral asked.

Amber returned it to the backpack, taking out the bracelets instead. She handed over the broken ones, keeping the intact one for herself. "I'm going into Cliffview with you. So you'll have to take at least three of us in, not two."

Morgane nodded. "We hoped you would, but didn't make plans for you in case you weren't interested. It'd be best if you could remove the bracelets for us."

"How many hybrids are in the village?" Amber asked.

"We'll be outnumbered," Gunsa said.

"Not once I start to break the bracelets," Amber

said. "You need to make sure you get your people out of there. Tell them to pack and be ready to leave."

"Someone will need to cause a distraction," one of Brigitte's hunters suggested.

Amber started to speak, breaking off when she noticed a large group of dragons headed towards them. "Are we expecting about thirty-five dragons?"

Ninian nodded. "They said they'd meet us here and come in close enough that the villagers will be able to reach them easily, but without any of them being noticed by the hybrids."

Jorn glanced skywards. "We need to go before it's too late."

Everyone readied themselves to leave. Dragons shapeshifted and hunters clambered onto their backs. Morgane stepped in front of Amber before she could clamber onto Treon's back. "Did you see Keeley?"

"Yeah. Both her and Ronan now have bracelets that they control."

"Thank you." Morgane paused a moment. "What is Ronan like?"

Amber struggled to think of something nice to say. After all, he was Morgane's father. "He's a survivor."

Morgane sighed. "That's how most people would describe Brigitte."

"He's not Brigitte." She wished she could say he was nothing like Brigitte, but that wasn't possible.

Morgane inclined her head before stepping back out of the way. "Thank you for all your help."

Not knowing what to say, Amber remained silent, giving a single nod before she clambered onto Treon's back.

They flew directly towards Cliffview, stopping nearby so everyone could get organised. They gave a head start to those who were to let the villagers on the outskirts know what was happening. The dragons Ninian had organised waited further back from the village in a forest clearing. They'd easily be able to take off from there once the villagers reached them.

Amber mentally searched the area again, having done so several times since they'd landed. No one was nearby. She turned to Treon who remained beside her. "Why can't we sneak in? You and the rest of the hunters could make us invisible."

Gunsa, not far from them, moved closer. "There are pillars embedded in some of the houses to prevent hunters from hiding themselves. Otherwise, we would have left years ago."

"Aren't they meant to be partially exposed?" Amber asked.

Gunsa nodded. "There are small vents that allow

the air into them. All the houses have them to make it impossible for people to easily find the houses that contain the rods."

"Time to go," Morgane said. "The majority of us will cause a commotion to draw as many hybrids to the one location as possible while Amber removes the bracelet of at least one of them. More if possible."

Amber doubted she'd manage more than one, unless they were scattered. She followed Gunsa, who led the way, the other hunter walking behind those of them playing at being hostages. She tried not to think of all the things that could go wrong, but there were so many of them that it was impossible to empty her mind of the many potential problems.

A hybrid stopped them before they could enter the village. "What are you doing back here so soon?"

"We were attacked and lost two hunters, but did manage to capture those who attacked. Or at least the ones who survived." Gunsa glanced at her hostages. "We need to take them to Brigitte and replace the hunters we lost."

"You should have taken them to Brigitte first." The hybrid remained in front of Gunsa, barring her way.

"I doubt she'd be up at this hour. Better to go there once the day has started," Gunsa said.

The hybrid remained where he was. "Who did you

need to replace the ones you lost? As soon as you have them, you can go to the castle. No waiting around for day."

"We've come a long way," Gunsa protested. "Surely-"

The hybrid interrupted her. "Who do you want?"

Morgane crossed her arms. "I am not travelling one step further. If Brigitte wants us, she can come and get us."

"Better to die in battle than to end up in one of her dungeons." Jorn threw himself at the hybrid, trying to tackle him to the ground. Within seconds hybrids ran towards them, drawing weapons.

Chapter Eighteen

Amber grabbed hold of the hybrid's arm before the rest could reach them, wrapping both hands around the bracelet, her companions helping hold him while she forced fireballs into the metal. She'd barely managed to break it when she was flung from him, landing on her back on the ground. Before she could rise to her feet, she was surrounded, needing to roll out of the way of an attack. She tried to turn into a goshawk, but ended up as a cat. She ran through the press of bodies as the hybrids tried to fend off one of their own.

Reaching the edge of the fight, Amber shapeshifted into her human form, grabbing hold of one of the nearby hybrids. She forced fireballs into his bracelet. He fought against her, drawing a dagger. She started to let go when Treon came to help her. Between the two of them she was able to break the bracelet, letting it fall to the ground. But she wasn't quick enough to get out of the way of another hybrid. She staggered back from the impact of his hit, barely avoiding a second attack.

Treon grabbed her arm, dragging her to the side. "Two will have to do. This is too dangerous."

Amber searched the area, noticing the fleeing villagers. Amongst them was a hybrid, escaping in the direction of Brigitte's castle. "One is getting away. We can't let him tell Brigitte who attacked."

Treon shapeshifted, taking to the sky. *"Where are they?"*

Amber tried to become a goshawk. This time she turned into a rat, needing to scurry out of the way of two fighting hybrids. It took two attempts before she could become a goshawk, needing to tell Treon she'd be with him soon and to fly towards Brigitte's castle.

Taking to the sky, Amber slipped past a sword blade, the hybrid bringing it down where she'd been. One of the hybrids who'd had their bracelet removed was lying lifeless on the ground, the other surrounded. He wasn't going to last long enough. *"Keep heading in the direction you're going, Treon."* She dived towards the ground. *"I'll catch up as soon as I can."* Landing behind a hybrid who was on the edge of the fight, she grabbed hold of his wrist, forcing fireballs against the metal band.

The hybrid drew a dagger with his free hand, trying to attack Amber.

She had to let him go to avoid being stabbed. It was impossible to grab hold of his arm again. He was too quick. Behind her the other hybrid died and she tried to become a goshawk and fly out of the area. She turned into a panther, launching herself at the hybrid since she was unable to fly out of his reach. Knocking him to the ground she quickly became human, grabbing hold of his arm.

The hybrid brought up the dagger, managing to get Amber in the side before the bracelet fell from his wrist.

She let go of him, rolling away as she pressed her hand against her side, healing herself. She didn't have time to stop. Another hybrid came for her. Struggling to her feet, she finally turned into a goshawk and flew above their heads, swooping several times to lure the freed hybrid to the rest of them.

Morgane flew in close, holding a bow. *"The plan was to flee once you removed the bracelets from two of them."*

Amber ignored her aches and pains, swooping on one of the hybrids at the edge of the fight. *"They'll* tell Brigitte who attacked. We don't want her to know. She might take it out on Ronan and Keeley." She swooped down on the hybrid several more times until he was far enough from the fight for her to land and become human.

"You've only just thought of that?" Morgane shot an arrow at a hybrid who headed towards Amber.

Grabbing hold of the hybrid's arm, Amber forced fireballs into him, relieved when two arrows struck him, distracting him from attacking her or pulling out of her grip. Within seconds the bracelet was on the ground and he was turning on his companions. Becoming a goshawk, Amber flew upwards, exhaustion tugging at her.

Landing several metres away, she became human and drew power from one of her bracelets. She was halfway through them and not likely to have any power spare to fill them. At least not any time soon. A sound had her spinning to face a hybrid who was late to the fight. She mentally scanned the area as she threw herself at him, several arrows sinking into his body as she grabbed hold of his arm. He fought against her grip as she forced fireballs against the metal band, stumbling back from him when it broke open.

She barely had the energy to shapeshift, squeaking

when she became a rat and had to scurry out of the way of the hybrid's feet. Racing towards the nearest cover, she again searched the area, relieved to find the hybrid had been distracted by bigger prey. His companions. Leaning against the wall of a building, Amber fought against exhaustion. Around her the village continued to empty. Off in the distance dragons flew from the clearing with two and sometimes three people on their backs. So far she couldn't sense any other hybrids nearby. Only the ones they'd been fighting. The one that had been flying towards Brigitte's castle was nowhere to be found and Treon was on the way back to Cliffview.

Several of Morgane's people returned to the village, attacking from above with bows. Amber forced herself to shapeshift, running towards the edge of the fight. She needed to release at least another two if they had any hope of taking out all the hybrids. Grabbing hold of one, she was knocked to the ground, dragged across it a few metres as she clung to his arm. She forced fireballs against the band, determined to hold on. If she let go, she wouldn't have another chance at this one. Not with how fiercely he tried to escape her. The bracelet snapped open and she let go of the hybrid. She landed on her back, rolling out of the way when he tried to attack her. It was impossible to rise to her feet with the way he focused his attention on her.

Treon swooped down and grabbed hold of Amber, flying upwards. *"Are you all right?"*

"I've been better." She pressed a hand against her ribs, healing them. The rest of her injuries were minor and could wait until after the fight. "Can you set me down on the far side of the hybrids?"

"Are you trying to get yourself killed?"

She couldn't resist smiling. She'd lost track of how many times she'd been asked that question. "Am I dead?"

"It won't be long with the way you're going."

"I know what I'm doing." Or at least she kind of knew what she was doing. Obviously adding a few extra animals hadn't been a good idea right now. "Set me down."

Treon flew down to where she wanted to be set down, becoming human and remaining at her side.

"What are you doing?"

"Assisting you," Treon stated.

She glared at him "You'll get yourself killed."

"Like you will?"

She made a noise that sounded very much like a dragon's growl, running towards the nearest hybrid. If he planned to stay at her side until she was finished, then she better get moving. Grabbing hold of the hybrid, she clung to him when he punched her in the ribs she'd just healed. Pain radiated through her and for a moment she couldn't cast fireballs.

Treon grabbed hold of the hybrid's other arm, preventing him from hitting Amber again.

She clung to the hybrid as he roared, trying to shake them off. It took a few seconds before she could force fireballs against the metal band. Fear raced through her when she did another search. The hybrid army was headed their way. The bracelet snapped open and Amber let go at the same time as she mentally spoke to those nearby. *"Army coming. We have to go."* She ran for cover, unable to shapeshift.

Before Amber could reach the building, Treon swooped down and scooped her up. *"How far away?"*

"If we're lucky, this lot will finish each other off before they arrive."

"Then we should stay and make sure of it," Becan said.

Treon landed well away from the fight, setting Amber down. *"They know where Gunsa has been stationed. We can't let any of them live."*

Amber staggered to her feet and dragged herself onto Treon's back. She drew power from another bracelet, energy filling her. "Okay. Let's take them out then."

Treon launched into the air, heading for the fighting hybrids. *"How close do you need to be to use your fireballs?"*

"About the same distance as your family with their bows." She could attack from further away, but closer was more accurate. And they needed accuracy and speed right now. The army was coming in faster than she'd expected. She counted the remaining hybrids as she threw fireballs at them. Four left and one of them was a hybrid without a bracelet. They could do this. If they hurried. Then it was three left, two and eventually only the one without a bracelet. He shapeshifted and took to the air. All those attacking swooped in on him. Amber slid off Treon's back at the movement, unable to keep her seat. She tried to shapeshift. Nothing happened. Spreading her arms wide, she reached for the hybrid's wing as she fell past it, grabbing hold of it and pulling him down with her.

"What do you think you're doing?" Treon demanded.

Clinging to the hybrid's wing as he struggled to maintain altitude, she got a better grip so she could draw one of her daggers, slicing into the membrane. *"Catch me when I let go."*

"This is madness," Treon said.

She heard the worry in his words. Trying not to

focus on her own worries and fears, she sheathed her dagger as she let go of the plummeting hybrid, trying to force herself to shapeshift into a goshawk. Before she could figure out if it was possible, Treon grabbed her out of midair, the action jarring through her. Below she sensed the hybrid die, the rest of those with them having followed him to the ground where they'd finished him off. *"We need to get out of here immediately. The army is only minutes away."* She sent the words to all those nearby.

"Everyone plans to meet up at our castle." Morgane took to the air, leading the way.

Amber wished she could ask Treon to set her down. She ached and hanging from his claws like this was making her dizzy. But the army was too close for them to stop. She'd wait until they put some distance between them and the village.

By the time they all reached Morgane's castle, it was after midday and Amber struggled to stay awake. It had been far too long since she'd slept. Her eyes felt gritty and it was an effort to keep them open. When she joined a group of them at a long table, the aged timber scarred and gouged, each time she blinked it took her longer to open her eyes.

"Once you've finished eating, I'll show you to where you can sleep," Treon thought to her.

"There's still a lot to do," Amber thought back to him.

He glanced at her where she sat beside him, smiling before returning to eating.

Amber felt like protesting again, even though she didn't know what she would be protesting against.

After the meal, Treon showed Amber to a room that overlooked a pond. There was very little in it, the large timber bed also in as bad a condition as the table. "We both need sleep. I'll be next door if you need me."

She started to ask him about having a wash, but there was no way she could stay awake that long. "Thank you."

Treon stepped closer, taking her hand. "No, thank you." He met her gaze. "For everything you've done for my family."

"It's for my family too. Brigitte has Ronan." She drew her hand from his, giving him a small, brief smile. "We have a common enemy."

"I believe it's more than that." He took a step towards the door. "I'll see you tomorrow."

Chapter Nineteen

Treon was gone before Amber could protest. Then she couldn't help wondering why she needed to protest. Treon and his family were likeable. She dropped onto the bed, the linen as worn as everything else, and stared at the ceiling trying not to think of everything that needed to be done. There was a lot. She filled one of her bracelets with the last of her power before she fell asleep, hoping nothing happened that she'd regret storing it.

Amber woke to thoughts of all the problems ahead of her, feeling only half rested. She'd used a lot of power… Her thoughts trailed off as she tried to figure out what day it was. The room was dark and she hurried to the window to look outside. Stars filled the sky and the moon was partially hidden by clouds. Had she slept several days? Or only part of one.

A sound had her spinning to face the door, her

hand half raised before she'd mentally searched the area. Discovering it was Treon, she lowered her hand before she'd finished turning to face him. "Is everything okay?"

"Nothing has changed."

She didn't know if that was good or bad. "What time is it?"

"Past the dinner hour." He remained in the doorway. "Are you hungry?"

"Yeah. Starving." She moved away from the window. "What happened to everyone from Cliffview?"

"Most of them are here." He stepped out of the doorway so she could leave the bedroom. "Some of them have family at Brigitte's other villages."

"What will Brigitte do to them?"

Treon shrugged. "We don't know for certain that she's been informed about their ties." He led the way through the castle.

"What do we know for certain?" Amber walked at his side, glancing into the rooms they passed. Some of them were filled with broken furniture and a layer of dust.

"That Brigitte doesn't know who attacked the village."

"How do you know that?"

Treon grinned. "Because she hasn't retaliated."

She chuckled. "Okay. That makes sense." Reaching the table, she turned to face him. "What do you and your family plan to do next?"

Treon shrugged. "They're still talking."

"You don't want to be part of the decisions?"

He grinned. "I have a feeling you will be a big part of the decision that is made. I'm not about to miss out on anything." He nodded towards the table. "You going to eat?"

Chuckling, she sat at the table. "What have they been thinking about doing? Are they going to rescue the rest of the villages?"

"Impossible." Treon sat beside her. "There's easily a hundred hybrids at the other two villages now. We've had dragons scouting and a couple are monitoring Brigitte's castle to see what she's up to."

"A hundred." Amber sighed heavily when he nodded. "How are we meant to take out a hundred of them? We barely managed the two dozen at Cliffview. Do you have more allies you can call on?"

"It's worse," Treon said.

She was half tempted to tell him not to say that. "How can it be worse?"

"She gave a dozen of her hybrids a hundred bracelets and told them to bring back more hybrids."

The food she'd eaten sat heavy in her stomach and she closed her eyes, trying not to think about how impossible everything seemed. Taking a deep breath, she opened her eyes to find that Treon watched her. "We need to take out the hunter and destroy the bracelets." There was no way they could survive if Brigitte put all her bracelets on hybrids.

"You can't expect to walk in there and take the bracelets," Treon stated.

Amber opened her mouth to agree, closing it instead as an idea came to her. Half formed thoughts raced through her mind. "I need to return to Brigitte's castle."

"What plan have you come up with?"

Amber shook her head. "None. Just ideas that might not work."

"I'll go with you."

"No–" She broke off when he placed his hand over hers. She glanced at his hand before meeting his gaze. "Treon–"

He interrupted her. "There's no guarantee you'll ever be able to return to your world. Ronan might not survive. Anything could happen."

She continued to meet his gaze. "No matter what happens, I'll never stop trying to return home. To all my people. Not just Kade." She slipped her hand out from beneath his, standing up. "Let your family know I'll be back later."

Treon stepped in front of her when she tried to leave. "Not on your own. It's too dangerous. I'll go with you."

She slowly shook her head. "You want more than I can offer."

Treon smiled briefly. "I might hope you'll change your mind, but I'd never force that change." He stepped to the side so she could pass. "I'll go with you."

She studied his face. She wanted to trust him. Was sick of doubting everyone's motives. "Okay."

Treon glanced over his shoulder. "Then we'd best go. Mum is determined to join us."

"Tell her we're only scouting and gathering information so I can see if any of my ideas might work." She hurried towards the exit, wishing she had time for a wash. That wasn't possible. Not with all that was going on. And especially not if she didn't want a group of dragons and hunters accompanying her. She doubted Morgane would come on her own.

Treon strode beside Amber. "Mum doesn't care. It's been too long since she's spoken to Keeley."

The bars of Keeley's cell came to mind. They'd be

perfect for her to test her ideas on. "Let her know that Keeley might be home before morning."

"What are you planning?" Treon stepped outside, becoming a dragon. *"That sounds like a little bit more than a scouting mission."*

"It's a fact finding mission." She clambered onto his back. "Do you know where Brigitte's hunter is?" Amber noticed that both Morgane and Jorn had nearly reached the castle's exit.

Treon took to the sky. *"No one has seen him in years."*

Again plans raced through her mind. "We need to find him. Need to make her show us where he is." Behind her she sensed Morgane and Jorn stop at the front of the castle. "What did you say to your parents?"

"That a small force can go where a large one can't. Now how do you plan to make Brigitte show us where the hunter is?"

Amber's lips slowly curved into a smile. "I'll track him down."

"You don't need to have met him to do that?"

"If we destroy all her bracelets, she'll need him to make her more. I can track where they've come from."

"Then why aren't we taking others with us so we can destroy the bracelets?" Treon slowed his pace.

"Because we need to find a way to get in and out without her noticing until it's too late." Amber mentally searched the area. They were alone. "Are you going to take me or am I going by myself?"

"I'll take you." He picked up his pace.

Amber's gaze was drawn to him, not sure what she heard in his voice. The thread of emotion beneath his words. She also wasn't sure she wanted to ask. Not after his earlier comments. So she remained silent. Which was becoming a habit lately.

The rest of the journey was silent, neither of them talking. Amber spent the time examining the forms she could now turn into, learning what a confusing mess she'd made of herself. She hadn't made much progress by the time they'd reached Brigitte's castle. She needed to shift between her various forms to make any real progress. Which was something she hadn't been game to do while on Treon's back far above the ground.

Treon bent the light around them as they drew close to Brigitte's castle. *"I can't reach Keeley. Is she still there?"*

Amber mentally searched the area. Once again Ronan was with Brigitte while Keeley remained in the same cell. She started to say the hunter-dragon was okay, but she changed her mind. She didn't know that for certain. All she knew was Keeley's location. "She's still in the same place. You need to go above the castle and fly to a point over the window before heading to the ground. There are more warriors than last time scattered about the castle grounds."

"I suppose that's to be expected after we stole all the people from one of her villages." Treon headed upwards, flying across the top of the castle before aiming towards the ground. *"How many more?"*

Amber automatically shrugged. "I dunno. Maybe double. Maybe a few more than that."

"Does that mean Keeley won't be home before morning?"

Amber grinned. "Not at all." She still had a theory to test and there were no warriors standing outside the hunter-dragon's cell window. When Treon landed on the ground beside the cell window, Amber focused on becoming a goshawk. It took far longer than it should, but at least she managed. She flew between the bars and landed on the floor, easily becoming human. At least she was able to turn into one of her forms without a drama.

Keeley struggled to her feet, staggering as she did so, pressing a hand against her side.

Shock raced through Amber as she dashed forward to support the hunter-dragon, her gaze taking in Keeley's many injuries. "Who did this?" She pressed a hand against Keeley's jaw.

Keeley brushed her hand away before she could heal the claw marks that ran across her cheek and over her jaw. "She'll know you've been here."

"She?"

Keeley stumbled back from her, drawing in a sharp breath. "Brigitte. Who else do you think would have done this?"

Amber grabbed hold of Keeley again, healing the marks on her face first. "You're coming with us." If her plan didn't work, she'd come up with another one. Brigitte had no reason to keep Keeley alive. Not like she had one to let Ronan live.

"How?" Keeley gestured towards the door. "There are warriors in the corridor. I can't make myself invisible. Not like Treon can."

Finished healing the worst of Keeley's injuries, Amber grinned. "Out the window." Letting go of Keeley, she strode towards it.

Keeley hurried after her. "I can't make myself smaller like you can. Or are you expecting the Pliethin to have given me that ability?"

Amber stretched out. The bars were just out of

reach. Jumping, her fingers brushed against them. A glance around showed there was nothing she could drag in front of the window to make it easy for her to reach them. "If I could grab hold of the bars, I'd widen them for you to go through." Or at least she hoped she'd be able to do that. She could only assume that the metals used for the bars was similar to what was available in the dragons' world and what Paili would have used for the barred window in her dungeon she'd put her and Ronan in when she'd captured them.

Keeley joined her by the window, cupping her hands. "I'll help you."

With a nod, Amber stepped onto the cupped hands, grabbing hold of the bars to keep herself from falling back down. She focused on one bar at a time, using fireballs to heat the metal and push it apart. When it gave, she nearly tumbled backwards.

A hand grabbed hold of hers, holding her in place. *"We should have brought rope,"* Treon thought to her.

Amber grinned up at him even though she couldn't see him, only sense him. "I didn't think of that. The window is a greater distance from the floor than I thought it was." She would have asked him to keep her invisible, while she did it from outside, but she didn't think now was the time to learn if casting fireballs would make them visible.

"How long will this take?" Keeley asked. "I can't hold you up for much longer."

Amber focused on heating the bar she still clung to, soon pushing it aside and creating a large enough gap for Keeley to get through. "You can let me go now, Treon." She dropped to the floor once he let go of her hand, cupping her own for Keeley. "Let's get you out of here."

"I'm not about to argue that statement." Keeley stepped onto her cupped hands and reached for the bars.

Treon's hands briefly appeared, grabbing hold of Keeley and drawing her upwards, making her invisible too.

Chapter Twenty

When Amber finally turned into a goshawk, she flew out of the cell and landed on Treon's back behind Keeley, remaining a goshawk. *"I need you to drop me close to Brigitte's window, then bring back as many dragons and hunters as you can. Along with sacks for them to put the bracelets in."*

"I'll go to the village. It's closest," Treon thought to the two of them.

"None of them are to keep any of the bracelets. I will destroy all of them. Understand?" Amber asked.

"None of them should be left in existence," Keeley stated. "You can start with destroying this one." She turned slightly so she could hold out her arm to Amber.

"Later. I don't want to waste any of my power. Who knows what might go wrong." She also didn't want to

shift out of her goshawk form with how difficult it was to change back into it.

Treon stopped outside the window. *"We'll be as quick as possible."*

"Thanks." Amber headed for the window ledge, changing direction when she realised Ronan and Brigitte were more than a little busy and she certainly didn't want to interrupt them. Not even in her cat form.

Perching on the roof, she mentally searched the area, following Treon and Keeley's path for a bit. Then she checked every other person she had a tie to, except Ronan, glad to find that they were all where she expected them to be. Everyone was safe. For now.

Two hybrids striding towards Brigitte's room drew Amber's attention back to Ronan. What had she missed? Had it been important? She tracked everyone's movements, including the hybrids who entered the room, ready to come to Ronan's rescue should he need her.

"I would have thought you'd take every opportunity for an egg," Ronan said.

"You think I'd allow you to spend the entire night beside me?" Brigitte demanded. "That I would trust you that much?"

"You didn't seem to have a problem the first night."

"Take him to the dungeon," Brigitte ordered.

Amber tracked Ronan as he was led away by the hybrids, flying to the cell window and slipping inside when they left him alone. She landed on the floor, becoming human. "Lover's quarrel?" She couldn't resist grinning.

"What are you doing here at this hour, Amber?"

She struggled to keep her grin in place at his tone and the use of her name. "Causing a few problems for Brigitte."

Ronan took a step towards her, his chains rattling. "They better not end up being problems for me. I've already told you I need a week."

"You'll probably get your week." Amber shrugged. "Possibly even longer." Who knew how long it'd take to find the hunter.

"I won't need longer. As soon as Brigitte has laid the egg, I'll be taking it and taking her home like I promised."

"Is there any way of getting out of keeping your promise?" She hated the thought of Brigitte loose in the dragons' world.

Ronan's lips curved into his predatory smile. "Just because I take her there doesn't mean it's her final destination."

"What are you planning?"

"No one will have a claim on my offspring that I can't trust to some degree. Clearly Brigitte isn't someone who can be trusted in the slightest."

"That doesn't tell me what you're planning." Sometimes she wished Ronan would say things plainly instead of avoiding them or hinting at things.

"Like you've told me what you're planning?"

She supposed he did have a point. Sighing heavily, she checked where Treon and Keeley were. She had plenty of time to tell Ronan everything that had been going on. They were still in the vicinity of the village. And they were still there when she'd finished explaining what had been happening to Ronan.

"I'm impressed, kitten. Maybe you aren't such a bad student after all."

Amber laughed softly. "I don't know that I'd go that far." Not with the amount of complaints she'd had from teachers over the years.

"Don't risk yourself to save another and I expect you back here every night around this time," Ronan said.

Relief rushed through her when she noticed Treon and Keeley were on their way back, too far from here for her to tell if they'd brought help. "I have to go. Treon is on the way back." And she certainly didn't need a lecture from Ronan. Like he could talk considering he was stuck in a dungeon.

Ronan grabbed her arm, preventing her from shapeshifting "Don't ignore what I said. You have a bad habit of trying to save everyone."

She thought of the hunter she'd stabbed, his brown eyes filled with surprise. "Not everyone."

"Are you having trouble sleeping?"

"No." She dragged her arm out of his grip. "I'm fine." If she hadn't been so exhausted, would she have had nightmares? She didn't know and hoped she didn't find out. At least not until she was back at Temolae Keep.

"Did you not say we're going to war?"

She shrugged, trying to figure out where he was going with his comment.

"There are always casualties in war. If they choose to fight, then they have to accept that death is one of the outcomes."

She thought of Gunsa. "What if they don't have any choice other than to fight for someone they hate?"

"Would you?" Ronan demanded. "Or would you find a way to escape or turn it to your advantage?"

"Not every situation is easily dealt with," Amber protested.

Ronan's predatory smile formed. "When have you ever done easy? Would you ever let anyone hold Kade or Crystal hostage?"

She felt her lips curve into a smile that mimicked his. "I'd like to see them try."

Ronan chuckled. "That's my kitten. Now go cause this bitch some pain. By the time we're finished with her she'll wish she was dead. Only then will I give her what she wants."

It was impossible for her to miss the promise in his tone and in his gold coloured eyes. "We are going home, not sticking around here playing games."

"Are we?"

She jabbed a finger at his chest. "I'm serious, Ronan." She sensed Treon and Keeley coming closer, wishing she could meet up with them before they reached the castle. She needed to deal with Ronan first. He couldn't be left thinking he could plan some elaborate payback for what Brigitte had done to him.

He captured her hand. "You think this won't have repercussions in our world?" He tightened his grip on her when she pulled away. "There are always repercussions. There are always problems. You need to think one step ahead of your enemy. Or more if possible."

She met his gaze, no longer trying to pull out of his grip. "I finished school last year."

"You fail the lessons I teach, you won't end up with a bad report card. You'll end up dead."

"Yeah well, I've already told you that isn't going to happen." She had too many people relying on her to keep them safe. "I need to go." She glanced at his hand that continued to hold hers. "I have things to do." Her lips again curved into the predatory smile he liked to use. "And a dragon to torment."

Ronan let go of her hand. "If only you could always think that way. Without giving into useless emotions like guilt."

She didn't bother to reply. There was no point. It was one thing they'd never agree on. Becoming a goshawk on her second try, she flew through the bars, heading towards Treon and Keeley. She was human. With human emotions. Ronan would have to learn to live with that.

Before Amber reached the hunter-dragons she could sense the dragons and hunters they'd brought with them. Eighteen. It might be enough. She tried not to let excitement build, but it was hard. They had a chance. This would weaken Brigitte's hold and she'd have no allies to follow her to the dragons' world.

Amber landed on Treon's back, behind Keeley who wore a dragon-leather backpack, and became human. "We need to take out the warriors guarding the window before I open the bars."

"Like last time?"

An agreement wouldn't come. All she could think of was Gunsa. What if the hunter was being forced to work for Brigitte? Ronan's words came to mind followed by brown eyes filled with surprise.

"Amber?"

She heard the concern in Treon's thoughts, but had no reassurances for him.

Keeley partially turned so she could meet Amber's gaze. "You're in pain?"

She took a deep breath before she answered. "We take them out like last time."

Keeley took Amber's hand. "Are you hurt?"

Amber stared at the hand that was delicate compared to Ronan's. "I will manage." She met Keeley's gaze again. "You don't need to worry."

Keeley lightly squeezed her hand, smiling slightly. "We are. Both of us. Now tell me what the problem is."

"How many hunters at Brigitte's castle are like Gunsa?"

Keeley studied her before answering. "No wonder

you intrigue my brother. If he wasn't so interested, I'd be interested myself."

"Ahh…" Amber's voice trailed off. She had no idea how to reply.

Keeley chuckled, a low, soft sound. "I know. Treon told me." She let go of Amber's hand to pat her brother's back a couple of times. "You're in a relationship with a dragon. What I can't understand is why you're here with Ronan and not your dragon."

"It's complicated." She managed not to add 'like everything related to dragons'. But it was close. Her gaze was drawn to the castle ahead of them. "I'll do what is necessary. You don't have to worry that I won't manage to do what has to be done."

"Where do you want those with us to wait while we take out the warriors guarding the cell window?" Treon thought to Amber.

She mentally searched ahead of them. "If we go straight to the window and they stop about ten metres from it and remain hidden, they won't run into any of the other warriors in the area."

"Will they see the warriors when we take them out?" Treon asked.

"Not as long as we stay close to the castle wall."

"How far exactly are ten metres?"

"Uhmm." She tried to think of a way to describe it.

"You're probably only ten to fifteen centimetres off two metres. Maybe five or six of you would be ten metres."

"I've let them know." Treon aimed for the ground in front of the cell window.

"Go to the right. We'll land beside them and slip around behind them. Hopefully, they're facing away from the castle," Amber said.

"It wouldn't make sense for them to watch the castle," Keeley said.

Amber turned into a goshawk as they drew near to the ground, giving herself extra time to change forms. It was worse than when she'd first become a Dragon Mage. She hated to think what Ronan would have said if he'd realised the problems she'd created for herself by adding extra forms she could shift into. She really needed time to practice.

She flew behind the hunter guarding the window, directing Treon to where the hybrid was, Keeley backing away from them so she wasn't in the way. Amber landed behind the hunter, becoming human and drawing her daggers, sinking them into him before he could turn and see Keeley who was now visible. Withdrawing her daggers, she slipped them back into her wrist sheaths. *"Hide them."* She turned her back on the bodies, trying not to think about yet more deaths.

Wrapping her hands around a bar, she heated it with fireballs, pulling it to the side and quickly doing the same to the other one. She clambered through the gap, dropping to the floor below. Remaining where she was by the window, she searched the area. The warriors guarding the door remained where they were. No one had heard or noticed anything. She looked up at the window where Keeley peered in at her. *"Tell everyone to remain quiet. There are warriors at the door."*

"I know. And only hunters will come in. We can remain unnaturally silent." Keeley dropped silently to the floor beside Amber, straightening and removing the dragon-leather backpack she wore.

Amber inclined her head, walking carefully with Keeley to a nearby crate and helping her fill the backpack. Others entered the cell, silently doing the same, the crates rapidly emptying as backpacks and sacks were filled. Some handed the filled backpacks and sacks through to those waiting outside and Amber kept track of everyone.

There was a group waiting in the nearby forest where two dragons and hunters carted the bagged up bracelets to, before returning for more. She wished they'd take them further away, but at least they were out of the castle and not within Brigitte's grasp. *"They will take them to your parents' castle, won't they?"* Amber thought to Treon and Keeley. She wished there was a way to track the bracelets. She didn't want anyone getting hold of them. They were too dangerous to let fall into the wrong hands.

"A dragon and hunter left the village at the same time as we did to bring back a group of dragons and hunters from my parents' castle to collect the bracelets," Treon thought to Amber, having remained outside.

She checked on Morgane, Jorn and their people, surprised to find most of them were on the way. *"They're coming. Your parents and their people."*

"You can sense them from here?" Keeley asked.

Amber nodded, filling a sack that Keeley held. She picked up the last bracelet in the crate, stilling when there was movement in the corridor. *"Something is happening."* She shoved the bracelet at Keeley before hurrying across the cell. She pressed her ear to the door, frowning at the sound of metal lightly brushing against metal. Shock raced through her when she realised she heard the sound of keys. Bringing fireballs to her hands, she forced them against the lock, making it impossible for the key to be used in it.

"Something's wrong." A warrior rattled the door.

"Give them to me." Another warrior demanded.

Amber stared at the lock when there was a scraping sound on the other side of it. She held her breath, listening for every movement and sound. The door remained shut.

"Here." The rattle of keys was more pronounced. "Wake Brigitte. Something's wrong." There was a short pause. "I can't contact the ones outside. You two get out there and find out what's going on. Take another four with you. Wake the barracks. Have the patrols increased."

Amber spun away from the door, mentally reaching for Keeley and Treon as she hurried across the cell. *"We have to go. Now. Everyone get out of here."*

"We've got one more crate to empty," Keeley protested.

Chapter Twenty-One

Amber tracked the warriors that had been ordered to check what was going on. She noticed other warriors had changed direction in their patrols and were headed towards them. *"We don't have time."*

"What if we haven't taken enough to make her have the hunter create more?" Treon asked.

Amber momentarily closed her eyes, trying not to let everything swamp her. She needed her own people. Needed Kade. Crystal. Rian. Even Daray. She knew what to expect of them. Knew what they were capable of. Drawing in a deep breath, she opened her eyes. *"Everyone possible needs to stay invisible. Get out of here as soon as you can and don't wait around for me."* As she thought the words to Treon and Keeley, she worked on trying to become a goshawk. She managed seconds after she finished giving them their orders, flying out the window. Sometimes she hated being right. A dozen Hell Hounds would probably be easier to face than what she was about to do.

"What are you planning to do?" Treon took to the sky, invisible as he followed her towards the incoming hunter and hybrid.

"Create a distraction."

"I can help," Treon offered.

"You need to get your people and the bracelets out of here," Amber ordered.

Treon remained at her side. *"I'm not about to leave you to face Brigitte's warriors alone. You mustn't think much of me if you believe I'd be willing to do that."*

If she'd been in human form, she would have sighed heavily. Bloody dragons! Did they have to take everything personally? Or as an insult? *"Fine. Then attack the hybrid when I distract the hunter."* She darted in and struck the hunter in the face causing him to stop bending the light around him and the hybrid.

Treon swooped in and snatched the hunter from the hybrid's back. The hybrid raced forward, barrelling into Treon and sending the three of them spiralling to the ground.

Amber flew towards the three of them, clawing at the wings of the hybrid who was grappling with Treon. Her attacks made no difference.

Treon's wings pumped the air and he let go of

the hunter as he fought the hybrid, struggling to halt their plunge towards the ground.

Amber was surprised at the relief she felt when another hybrid swooped in and grabbed the hunter, stopping his free fall to the ground. She shouldn't have been relieved. They were the enemy and now there were two hybrids for her and Treon to face. Searching out Keeley and the rest of the dragons and hunters collecting the bracelets, she found that some of them were still in the cell, a couple of hunters waiting outside the window. They needed to hurry. She could sense more of Brigitte's hunters and hybrids coming towards her and Treon. Soon they'd be outnumbered.

The second hybrid left the hunter on the ground and arrowed towards Amber. Fear exploded through her when hybrids poured out of the front of the castle. They'd be attacking her and Treon within minutes. If she didn't do something drastic, the two of them would be surrounded and dead within seconds of their arrival.

The hybrid swiped at her, roaring when she dodged his attack.

She threw herself at him, becoming human and drawing a dagger to shred his wing, clinging as he rolled, trying to dislodge her. She barely held on, throwing herself from him when he headed for the ground, one wing not working properly. She struggled to change form, the ground coming closer as she tried to keep the panic at bay. Focusing on the goshawk, she changed shape to glide upwards, heart racing and trying not to think about how close she'd come to colliding with the snow-covered ground. She doubted the snow would have done anything to break her fall.

"What are you doing, Amber?" Treon thought to her.

The familiar demand would have made her smile if she'd been human. Landing in front of the hybrid, she became human, grabbing hold of his wrist and forcing fireballs into the bracelet before he had a chance to react to her move.

He drew his sword, drawing it back.

Amber clung to the bracelet, forcing more fireballs into it, ready to let him go as the sword came closer. About to let go, not crazy enough to risk being struck by the sword, the bracelet opened and she stumbled back, letting it drop to the ground. The sword passed by harmlessly, the air of its movement brushing across her.

The hybrid looked at her, confusion crossing his face as the sword fell from his hands, landing in the snow with a thud. He looked from Amber to the sword once more.

Not waiting for him to shake off the effects of the bracelet and attack her, Amber ran after the hunter who was heading towards the castle. She tackled him to the ground. "Do you follow Brigitte willingly?"

The hunter struck out at her, trying to draw a dagger with his other hand. "What sort of question is that?"

She drew the dagger before he could, throwing it out of reach. "A good one. Now answer the question."

"Why would I follow someone who's weak? She's the strongest leader in the country." Overpowering her, he rolled, pinning her to the ground. "Weak." The word was clearly an insult.

Amber mimicked Ronan's predatory smile, trying to ignore the cold of the snow against her back. "That's just what I needed to hear." For once, the panther came easily, going for his throat, drenching her in blood. She padded away from the body, leaving bloody footsteps behind her. A quick mental search showed the hybrid she'd set free now attacked the ones that had arrived, Keeley and those with her were headed for the group waiting in the forest and Morgane and Jorn weren't far away. The main problem was that Treon was rapidly being surrounded. *"Go invisible, Treon."*

"Then they'll focus on you." He continued to fight the hybrids that came at him.

"They'll have to catch me first. Don't argue or I'll leave you here to die." She doubted she would, but he didn't know that. It took her several attempts to become a goshawk, the rat wanting to break free. That was the last thing she needed. Streaking towards him, she felt a small amount of relief when he vanished. Only a small amount since the hybrids turned their attention on her when Treon flew up out of their reach and they were unable to find him.

"You wouldn't leave me to die. You don't have it in you." There was humour in Treon's thoughts. *"Weren't you going to flee?"*

She darted between hybrids, avoiding claws and barbed tails. *"Fly in the opposite direction of your people and become visible once you're several metres from the hybrids."*

"What are you planning?"

"Escape, of course." She checked where everyone was. Morgane and her people hadn't reached the ones in the forest yet. They weren't far off though. A gust of wind buffeted her and she nearly ran into a barbed tail. Flying upwards, she dodged another gust

of wind, flying at the hunter who had sent them at her. She angled away from him when a hybrid tried to attack her.

"They're not taking the bait," Treon thought to her.

"Give them a chance." She flew towards Treon, pushing herself to go as fast as possible. She knew the moment they went after Treon, sensing them all move towards him. She dropped down on one of the hybrids at the edge of the horde, the other hybrid she'd freed now dead. If she could free another one, it might be the distraction they needed to escape. A mental search of the area had her heart race faster. More hybrids flew towards them, amongst them Brigitte. They didn't have long. Becoming human, she tried to shred his wing.

He rolled, first in one direction and then in the other, shaking her from him.

She lost her grip, grabbing hold of a wing, hacking at it with the dagger she held before she once more lost her grip. Letting go of the dagger, she struggled to change forms. Before she could, the hybrid grabbed her from the air only metres from the ground, his claws sinking into her skin. Twisting in his grip, she tossed fireballs at him. He let her go and she crashed the couple of metres to the ground, the chill of the snow sinking into her body as the air was knocked from it.

The hybrid landed in front of Amber, becoming human and drawing two daggers. He grinned. "Thought you could ground me?"

She gasped in a lungful of searing cold air, unable to move due to the pain radiating through her. All she could think was that at least he'd broken her fall.

"Amber! Get up. What are you doing?" Treon thought to her.

She sensed him changing direction, heading back towards her. *"Get out of here. Don't bring them back to me. I've got this under control."* She didn't know how she moved, but somehow she rolled out of the way of the booted foot that came for her.

The hybrid growled, throwing himself at her, his dagger aimed for her heart.

She twisted enough that his dagger sank into the snow to the side of her and grabbed his wrist, forcing fireballs into the metal band.

The hybrid laughed. "Don't you know we love fire? You are pathetic."

She grinned up at him as the bracelet snapped open. "Am I?" Catching the fleeting look of confusion on his face, she pushed against him, slipping out from under his weight, she snatched up her dagger that was only metres from where she'd landed and ran in the same direction Treon had taken. *"Go invisible, Treon."* Sheathing the dagger, she tried to become a goshawk, sensing the hybrid was gaining on her.

"What are you doing? Change form and get out of there," Treon thought to her.

She was trying, but she wasn't about to let him know that. She finally changed form, but not into the one she wanted. The panther was faster at running than a human, even a hybrid one and she loped across the snow-covered ground, putting more distance between them. Above, hybrids changed direction to head towards her, hunters sending gusts of wind at her, stirring up the snow and shaking clumps of it from tree limbs. She dodged the clumps as they fell, leaping over swirling snow rather than risk they were hiding some danger.

"Amber! Look out."

She didn't need Treon's warning. She sensed the hybrid diving towards her. She leapt out of the way and he pulled up at the last second. Not that it mattered. The hybrid who had been following her attacked him and she was able to run without needing to worry about the two of them. A mental search of the area let her know Morgane and her people had finally arrived and the villagers were leaving. It didn't make her feel in the slightest bit relieved. What if they tried to come and help? Getting the bracelets away was a priority.

Another hybrid swooped down on Amber, fainting with claws before swinging the barbed tail towards her.

Pain exploded through her side, the scent of her blood overpowering that of the hunter's blood that coated her. She stumbled, tumbling across the ground to come to a stop at the base of a tree, becoming human. Pressing a hand against her side, she healed herself as the hybrid landed in front of her, staying in wyvern form. She focused on the goshawk, trying to shift forms.

The hybrid swung its barbed tail towards her.

Her gaze was focused on the barb. There was no room to move. A tree was to her side, the barb coming from the other side. Fear burst through her, rapidly followed by anger. She wasn't about to die in some strange world. Seconds before the barb struck her, she became a goshawk, taking to the sky and darting through the crowd of hybrids towards Treon who demanded she answer him. Dizzy with relief, she could only focus on avoiding the attacking hybrids and hunters.

"Amber. Please. Are you unharmed?" Treon thought to her.

She flew above him, landing on his back and seeing the light bend around her as she came to a rest, becoming human. She clung to him, heart still racing. "Go home, Treon." Leaning forward she wrapped her arms around him, not certain her legs would be enough to help her remain on his back. Exhaustion and pain tugged at her and she closed her eyes. She'd heal herself soon. Once she'd caught her breath.

"Are you unharmed?" Treon persisted.

"I can heal myself."

"Then why haven't you?"

A weary smile briefly formed. "Take me to your home, Treon. Before I'm too exhausted to hold on."

"You shouldn't have done all that you did. It was too much for you."

Again a smile formed. This one less weary, his words reminding her of similar comments. "Obviously it wasn't. We survived, didn't we?"

"Barely."

"Did your family get all the bracelets?" She didn't have the energy to reach further away to speak mind to mind with anyone.

"They have them. All of them. Except one. Keeley left it on an upturned crate in the middle of the room."

Amber laughed, a smile remaining behind. "I like your sister."

"She likes you too."

"Ahh, yeah." She didn't like Keeley in quite that way. A wave of humour washed over her from Treon.

"I'm glad I'm not the only one who causes that tone in your voice."

"I'm flattered, but-"

Treon interrupted her. *"You're waiting for someone."*

"Not at all. There isn't any waiting involved. I'm working on getting home to him."

"Is he worthy of you?"

She didn't hesitate. "Yeah. He is." She relaxed against him.

"Don't fall asleep."

Her eyes closed. "You need saddles."

"We had a look for them, but there isn't much left in the castle."

"I'm sorry."

"Don't be. What you've done is better than any sympathy."

Chapter Twenty-Two

With her eyes still closed, Amber healed some of her wounds, smiling at Treon's words. They were a typical dragon statement. She couldn't help wondering how hunters saw things and if the dragon overpowered what they were like.

By the time they reached Morgane and Jorn's castle, the sun was well and truly up and Amber was barely conscious. She staggered when she clambered off Treon's back.

Treon shapeshifted, scooping her up and striding towards the entrance with her.

"Put me down. I can walk."

Treon looked her over, continuing to carry her. "You look like you need a wash."

"I don't suppose you have hot running water."

"Not these days." He changed direction, going around the castle instead of inside it.

"What are you doing?" Amber made a half-hearted attempt to get out of his arms. She was so exhausted there was a good chance she'd collapse before she'd walked far.

"Stay still. You're not the only one feeling the fight."

She pressed a hand against his chest, giving him a general heal since she didn't know what was wrong with him.

"Stop it. What are you trying to do to yourself?"

She frowned. "I don't get what you mean. I was healing you, not me."

"Exactly. Don't you have any sense of self preservation?"

"Of course I do, but you said-"

Treon interrupted her. "You would exhaust yourself to heal someone with only minor wounds."

How many times had she heard that complaint? Amber grinned. "I'm a healer."

"Something about that amuses you?" Treon set her down beside the pond.

"You're not the first who's commented on it." She stared at the water. "This is not where you expect me to wash." It might be warmer here than at Brigitte's castle, but the air was still cool.

"The other option is a wooden tub in front of a fireplace."

She looked between the castle and the pond, sighing heavily. "I miss showers, running water and flushing toilets." The medieval bathroom facilities left a lot to be desired. "And commercial toilet paper."

"Maybe one day you can show me your world."

She met his gaze, not sure what to tell him.

He held out a hand. "As friends."

She hesitated. "Friends." She couldn't help the uncertainty in her tone.

He grinned. "For now. I'll see if your Kade truly is worthy of you."

She took his hand, holding onto it as she continued to meet his gaze. "He's probably more worthy of me than I am of him." She brought with her the kind of baggage that was bad for a dragon's health.

"I find that hard to believe."

"My grandparents are knights."

"They're warriors?"

She laughed, letting go of his hand. "Yeah, but not the sort a dragon wants to meet. They're the kind of knights that have spent a lot of their life hunting and killing dragons."

"And yet you ended up with a dragon."

"Yeah." She faced the pond, drawing in a deep

breath. "I suppose I should get this over and done with." The blood had dried on her skin and clothes and felt terrible. A sound had her spinning to face the castle, her hands half raised before she realised it was Keeley coming towards her. She lowered her hands. In her exhaustion she'd stopped regularly searching her environment. She had to be more vigilant. She didn't know this world. Her gaze was drawn between the siblings. Although she was beginning to think some of the inhabitants could be trusted.

Keeley carried a bunched up armful of material that she set at the water's edge. "To wrap around us once we've cleaned up a bit." She strode into the pond, breathing in sharply. "I forgot how cold the pond always is."

Amber took a step back from the water. "Great."

Treon chuckled, following his sister into the water. "You would face life-threatening situations without hesitation yet baulk at a little cold water."

Her gaze scanned the pond. "It isn't exactly little."

"Smaller than the Great Lake," Treon said.

Holding her breath, Amber followed the siblings into the water. She let her breath out in a rush at the chill that seeped into her. "Tropical holiday." She muttered the words under her breath, like a mantra. They didn't help.

"You ended up in the wrong country if you're looking for the tropics." Keeley strode for the bank, water streaming down her body as she exited and reached for a large cotton towel.

Amber ducked beneath the water, washing the blood from her hair before she rose. She looked at the siblings that were now both on the bank, Treon holding out a towel to her. "No. This is the right country." Leaving the water, she took the towel and wrapped it around herself. She had no idea what would happen next or what Treon might think of Kade, but she was glad Ronan had brought her here. "You don't deserve what Brigitte is doing to you."

Keeley slung an arm around her shoulders. "I could so easily fall in love with you. I have a weakness for those who want to right all the wrongs." A sigh escaped. "A pity their lives always end so badly."

Amber leaned against Keeley as they headed towards the castle, Treon walking on the other side of her. It was an effort to keep moving. "That isn't about to happen to me."

"Good," Keeley stated.

Amber yawned, having been about to ask Keeley why she thought that.

"I'll organise food and clothes for you so you can

get to bed." Keeley pulled away from Amber, hurrying ahead of them.

Amber wasn't even tempted to protest. A smile briefly appeared as she wondered what Rian would have said about her not arguing over someone taking care of her. An ache formed in her chest as thoughts of Rian made her think of Crystal and then Kade. Ronan better not make her wait long or she'd find her own way home to them. Somehow.

After she'd dressed in clean clothes and eaten, Amber fell instantly asleep. Not that it helped for long. She was woken several times by dreams of blood. Oceans of it. Each time she forced herself back to sleep, trying to focus instead on those in her life she loved and couldn't imagine living without.

She finally dragged herself out of bed late in the evening, asking if there was a hunter and dragon who could take a message to Ronan for her. There was no way she could fly there or even remain seated on Treon's back if he flew her there. She was still too exhausted.

She spent the evening in her room focusing on each of the animals she could change into, not trying to shift, just learn them. Trying to return to a more normal sleeping pattern, Amber tried to go to bed around midnight after a late dinner and a return message from Ronan that he expected her the next night, not a messenger. Again her sleep was broken and she prowled the bedroom in the early hours of the morning, as dawn approached, light slowly brightening the room.

The day was filled with destroying bracelets, storing some of her power and practising shifting into her various forms. Taking out the hunter, who made the bracelets, wasn't going to be easy. From what little she'd learned from Keeley, the ancient hunters, the ones alive way past what those of their kind typically lived due to the help of dragon blood, were far more powerful than the modern ones with their diluted bloodlines. She didn't know what that meant, but assumed she was in for a major battle.

Making sure she didn't overdo things, she spent plenty of time resting throughout the day. She headed for Brigitte's castle after dinner, taking Treon up on his offer of giving her a ride. He landed by the window of Ronan's cell and she jumped off his back, landing on the ground as a cat. Not what she'd planned to turn into. But at least she'd instantly turned into something. That had to be progress, right? She didn't have a clue.

Slipping through the bars, she leapt lightly to the floor of the cell, becoming human as she stopped in front of Ronan. She drew in a sharp breath as she caught sight of him, reaching for his face.

He caught her hand before she could make contact with the claw mark that ran across his cheek and over his jaw. "Don't, kitten. Think, don't react. How would I explain you healing me?"

"Brigitte did this?" Anger and a warning filled her tone.

Ronan's predatory smile formed. "Feeling protective of me, kitten?"

She stepped close to him, not needing to tilt her head up much to maintain eye contact with him. "Are you not mine, Ronan?"

"As much as you're mine, Amber."

"Then how did you think I'd feel when I saw what she's done?"

"Are you sure you won't have kids with Rian?"

"He's not interested in me." She couldn't help thinking about Treon.

Ronan studied her. "Who is?"

She grinned. Trust him to have picked up on her tone. "It doesn't matter. I'm not interested in any of your children or grandchildren."

"Grandchildren. The boy is interested in you?"

"Was there a reason you demanded I be here? I

doubt it was to talk about me having kids with one of your descendants."

"She wants to know what your plans are."

"Brigitte?"

Ronan nodded. "Why do you think she tortured me?"

"Ronan." She pulled her hand out of his grip, reaching for his shirt.

He captured both her hands. "You can't heal me, kitten. I don't exactly go to her bed fully clothed."

"You're an idiot."

His grip tightened on her. "Be careful what you say, kitten."

"Well, you are. Why sleep with the woman who's tortured you? That sounds like the makings of a really bad relationship."

"I only want one thing from her and it isn't a relationship."

"Gold offspring," Amber said.

"Do you have a problem with that, kitten?"

She had no idea what to say. From all she'd seen, he hadn't made a very good father. Did she really want to help him gain another child? "I guess we'll have to wait and see if I do have a problem."

Ronan's gaze narrowed. "Don't push it, kitten.

Now what have you been doing and why weren't you here last night?"

She briefly told him, avoiding any mention of the difficulties she'd been having shapeshifting. Hopefully, he'd never need to know. When he remained silent, she asked, "Do you need anything?"

He shook his head. "I'll see you tomorrow night."

"Okay." She'd nearly reached the window, having been struggling to become a goshawk, when he spoke.

"A small favour."

She turned to face him, frowning. "I owe you another favour?" What lame excuse had he come up with this time?

"No. I offer you a small favour."

She stared at him, closing her mouth when she realised it was ajar. He would owe her a favour? And she hadn't needed to hassle him to agree? "Are you okay?"

"Don't be smart, kitten."

She hadn't been. She'd been seriously worried about him. She changed her mind about clarifying her comment. "I'll see you tomorrow night." She held his gaze a moment, thankful that when he nodded, she was finally able to turn into a goshawk and fly between the bars of the window to land on Treon's back.

"Is everything all right?" Treon flew back towards his parents' castle.

Amber became human, trying not to think about all the problems. "It will be." She wouldn't accept anything else.

The next three days went by in a blur of sameness. Amber filled her jewellery with power, practised shapeshifting, destroyed more bracelets and visited Ronan late each evening. Every night he looked worse than the previous. On the third night she demanded, "Is it worth this?" She made a vague gesture towards him.

"You should know better than to ask that question. Gold is everything in our world."

She started to automatically protest that it wasn't her world. She remained silent. It was her world too. Sometimes it was still hard to believe that. "Surely she still can't think you know where I am and what I'm up to."

Ronan gave Amber a look to let her know it was a ridiculous statement. "She sent two dozen warriors to a place she called 'the nest' to escort a shipment of bracelets."

"Finally." She'd begun to think Brigitte wasn't

interested in having more brought to her castle. That she might store them elsewhere.

"Don't go doing anything stupid," Ronan warned.

"I don't plan to so you can stop telling me that."

"Do you ever plan to?"

There was no way she could answer that question without incriminating herself. "I should go. Your daughter will want to hear this news."

Ronan nodded, not speaking until Amber reached the window. "I've decided there is something I want you to do."

"What is that?"

"I want to meet Treon."

"Now?" She was tired from destroying bracelets and she still had more to go.

"Next time." He paused a moment. "Weren't you going?"

With a single nod, she became a goshawk. She took to the skies where Treon flew in slow circles well above the castle since there'd been too many warriors guarding the place. She landed on his back. *"A shipment of bracelets is due any day and Ronan wants to meet you."*

"Is that a problem?" Treon asked.

Becoming human, she shrugged, even though

Treon couldn't see her. "Anything is possible. It is Ronan after all."

"I want to meet him anyway."

"Why?"

"Mum wants to know more about him. I need to know that he isn't going to hurt her like Brigitte has."

"He won't want to kill her for her heart, or anything like that. But he probably will want to use her to his advantage." She was pretty sure Ronan would be annoyed if he ever learned she'd warned Treon, but after the way they'd taken her in and accepted her, she couldn't let him meet Ronan without a warning.

"He's your ally."

She laughed. "Yeah, but I don't have any illusions about him and what he's capable of." Although she still couldn't understand why he remained with Brigitte when she tortured him every day. Even for the chance of a Gold offspring that seemed pretty excessive. Her hand curled into a fist as she thought of the wounds on him that he wouldn't let her heal. There was no way she wanted Brigitte anywhere near her world. Ronan needed to find a way to get out of keeping his promise.

Chapter Twenty-Three

When they arrived back at Morgane and Jorn's castle, Amber retreated to the room she used, filling her daggers and sword with power. She glanced around, looking for other things she could store it in. There was nothing. She needed more jewellery. Needed more weapons. And needed more stored power. Closing her eyes, she tried not to be overwhelmed by everything. Slow, steady breaths didn't help. She needed to get Ronan away from Brigitte before she killed him. And she ended up stuck in this world.

She drew in another deep breath. No matter what he said, once she took out the hunter, she was getting him out of there. Even if she had to knock him out to do it. A smile formed, one that was similar to Ronan's predatory one. Or heal him so he had no choice other than to leave. The pressure on her chest eased and breathing became a little easier. He would be annoyed, but that was too bad. It was time to get him out of there.

Feeling less overwhelmed, Amber headed to bed, not dreaming for once. It wasn't until late afternoon that the dragon and hunter that were keeping watch on Brigitte's castle arrived to let them know that the hybrids had brought in several crates of bracelets.

The hunter finished by saying, "We wasted our time taking all those bracelets from her and destroying them."

"Not at all." Amber turned to Treon. "Interested in checking things out with me?"

"Yes."

Morgane rested a hand on Treon's shoulder. "The two of you can't go alone."

Amber took a step towards the exit. "We aren't going to attack anyone. I'm just tracking the hunter down." Her lips curved into a smile similar to Ronan's predatory one. "Then we'll need an army to take him down. Think you can organise that?"

Jorn slipped his arm around Morgane's waist, drawing her close. "For something like taking Brigitte's hunter out, I know a lot of people who'd want to be involved."

"Good." With a glance at Treon, Amber strode

outside, clambering on his back when he followed and stopped in front of her to become a dragon.

They headed straight to Brigitte's castle and Amber checked in the cell where the bracelets had been stored. It was empty. Not even the crates had been left in there. Becoming a cat, after several attempts, she roamed through the castle checking every room and space for where the new crates were stored. There were several places she couldn't enter, even as a rat, and one place that seemed likely considering the amount of warriors stationed in the corridor outside the locked door. It was in a tower room, the windows boarded up and only the one access.

She made her way to Ronan's cell, planning to ask him to take her into the room through the Void. Becoming human once she jumped through the window and landed on the floor, shock raced through her. She hurried to Ronan's side where he was collapsed on the floor, his blood stained body only half clothed and the bruises and cuts covering his torso making her chest ache.

He grabbed her hands when she placed them on his chest, his grip tightening on them. "Don't."

"Are you hoping to die?"

His predatory smile made a brief appearance. "Have I ever come across as suicidal to you, kitten?"

"No." But then he'd never reunited with an old lover. At least not as far as she knew. "Ronan, you can't keep letting her do this to you." She tried to break his hold on her, desperately wanting to heal him.

"Why are you here? This isn't the usual hour you visit."

She drew in a deep breath, momentarily closing her eyes as she lowered her head. "It doesn't matter." Raising her head, she met his gaze. "You're a mess."

"What do you want, Amber?" His tone was sharp.

"I can't enter a room that might be where the bracelets are kept. I was hoping you could use the Void to enter it."

Letting go of Amber's hand, Ronan struggled to rise.

She clasped her hands together rather than reach for him, her jaw tightening on words she shouldn't speak.

He swayed on his feet. "Where is it?" He held out a hand.

She held onto his hand, wanting to slip an arm around his waist and support him. "In one of the towers."

Ronan brought the bracelet to his lips, whispering against it before taking them into the Void.

"I was going to ask Treon to keep watch in case someone tries to enter your cell so you can return," Amber said.

"And how were you expecting him to contact you while you're in the Void? It's not like they have phones here." Ronan walked through the cell wall and along the corridor.

Amber wished it wasn't such slow going walking through the Void. It took them ages to reach the corridor where they stopped in front of a heavily guarded door. She looked between it and Ronan, worried he might pass out. "Are you sure-"

"How else do you think you'll get into that room if I don't take you?"

She slipped an arm around his waist, tightening her hold on him when he tried to pull away. "Don't be an idiot, Ronan. If you collapse, I don't want to get stuck in the Void."

They walked through the warriors guarding the door and into the room. Ronan leaned heavily on Amber. "Now what?"

She stared at the dozen warriors stationed around the room guarding the open crates of bracelets. "Over by the boarded up window. We only have to come out of the Void long enough to grab one and that spot is far enough from the lantern they might not notice us. Or if they do only think they're imagining things."

Ronan gave a look that let her know he didn't think much of her plan. He walked towards the spot she'd indicated, reaching out a hand for one of the bracelets. They were out and back in the Void in a matter of seconds, Ronan holding the bracelet.

The room erupted in chaos, warriors running towards the location only to look around and demand what was going on.

"Get us out of here." Amber took the bracelet from Ronan as he took them through the Void to his cell. She felt the place it had come from as they stepped out of the Void. "Can you take me to the hunter?"

"None of this better interfere with my plans," Ronan warned.

She looked him up and down. "I don't think much of your plans."

Ronan took them back into the Void. "Where are we going?"

At the weariness in his voice, she studied him, anger racing through her. "She will die." Brigitte didn't deserve to live. She was too dangerous.

"In time, kitten. In time."

Amber focused on the destination. "I'm ready."

Ronan took them through the Void again,

remaining in it when they arrived. They were in a cave filled with hybrids who were working on making more bracelets. "Now what?"

"I need to find out where we are in the world."

Sighing, Ronan took them through the cave, stepping outside onto the slopes of a snow-covered mountain and away from the opening before he left the Void.

Amber searched for all those she knew. "We're not far from Brigitte's castle." Her mouth dropped open as she realised what was in the area. She faced the cave. "It's full of wyverns. Hybrids and wyverns."

"Are you sure?" Ronan asked.

"The nest." It made sense. "It has to be not only where the bracelets come from, but also where the hybrids are bred." She searched the cave, trying to find someone who wasn't wyvern or hybrid. Or even dragon since there were a few of them. "I can't–" She broke off when she sensed someone that seemed like they barely made any impression. Like they were almost invisible.

"You can't what?" Ronan asked.

"I found him." And the power that surrounded him felt like a bottomless well. She had no idea how they were to take him out.

"Do we take care of him before we leave? I can take

you through the Void and we can come out behind him," Ronan suggested.

Amber shook her head. "He's too powerful for that." She needed to come up with a plan. Except she was all out of ideas.

"We can return to Brigitte's castle now?" Ronan asked wearily.

She strengthened her ties with the hunter. "Yeah." She should be able to find him no matter where he went.

Ronan took them through the Void, coming out in the cell only to collapse on the floor.

Dropping the bracelet she held, Amber knelt at his side, placing her hands against his bare chest. "Ronan." She willed him to open his eyes as she healed him.

He grabbed hold of her hands as his eyes opened, staring up at her. "Enough. Any more and she'll know."

"You seriously aren't going to take her home after what she's done to you."

"A promise must be kept."

"But she's tortured you." She wanted to shake him.

"The torture is a separate matter."

"What matter? Why is she continuing to do this to you?"

Ronan held her gaze. "Refusing to give her details about you."

"Ronan-"

He cut off her anguished cry. "This has nothing to do with you."

"How can you say that?"

"My secrets are my own, and I refuse to share them with anyone. Especially if that person thinks they can force them out of me."

His words brought a reluctant smile to her lips. The comment was so him. Her smile faded. "You're going to get yourself killed."

He remained on the floor, looking up at her. "Would you miss me, kitten?"

She had no idea how to answer him. Before she could come up with a reply, she heard rapidly approaching footsteps. She scooped up the bracelet and snapped it around her other wrist before changing into a rat, surprised she changed so quickly. She scurried across the floor, searching for a crack to hide in as the door swung open.

Ronan remained on the floor, staring up at Brigitte and the two accompanying hybrids. "Miss me already, Bri?"

Amber had no idea how he managed to dredge up a smile. She wanted to burst out of hiding and attack

Brigitte when she pressed a foot against Ronan's chest.

"You want to be careful how you talk to me, Ronan." She leaned forward, pressing down on his chest. "After tonight I might not need you any longer."

"There's no guarantee the hatchling will be Gold," Ronan said.

Brigitte shrugged, turning away from him. "Fetch me another bracelet. I want to be certain that his is working." She again looked down at Ronan. "And I will replace it every day to make sure you can't interfere with it."

"What are you going on about?" Ronan demanded.

"My warriors said they saw you in one of the rooms upstairs."

"Then why am I back here?" Ronan remained on the floor.

"That's what I'd like to know." Brigitte studied Ronan. "And I will find out." She strode towards the door, pointing to one of the hybrids. "You stay here and watch him." She glanced at Ronan. "I'll be back to put the bracelet on you once I deal with the incompetents that arrived."

Amber mentally searched the castle, finding a group of hybrids entering it. With them was a dragon. One she didn't recognise. She mentally reached for Ronan, finding that he must have activated the bracelet.

The hybrid left behind in the cell closed the door, standing in front of it with his arms crossed over his chest.

Amber scurried across the floor to Ronan's side. She placed a paw against his hand, trying to reach him.

Ronan rolled onto his side, his back to the hybrid, and raised the bracelet to his lips. *"What do you want, kitten?"*

"You need to leave."

"Not yet. One more day. Come for me tomorrow night." He scooped her up, staggering to his feet.

"Come on, Ronan. It's crazy to stay here."

He carried her to the window and set her down on the ledge. *"Tomorrow night. No matter the results, I'll be leaving then."*

She remained on the ledge when she would have preferred to jump to the ground and scurry as far from the cell as possible before Brigitte could return. *"Come with me. Please, Ronan. Don't stay with her any longer."*

"I'll see the plan through to the end."

"What are you doing over there?" the hybrid demanded.

"Setting it free." Ronan raised the bracelet to his lips, his back still to the hybrid. *"Tomorrow, kitten."* He lowered his arm before facing the hybrid. "Why? Did I let your dinner escape?"

When the hybrid growled, Amber tried to reach Ronan, but the bracelet was once again active. She glared at him, wishing she could have told him not to stir his guard. But it was Ronan. He often did things that most wouldn't consider doing. Reaching the edge, she stepped over it, becoming a cat before she landed on the ground. Excitement burst through her. She might finally be getting the hang of all the animals she could turn into.

It didn't take her long to find Treon and he collected her, dropping to the ground so she could race up his leg and land on his back, not becoming human until he'd taken to the air. She told him what had happened during the flight back to his parents' castle. At least the information relevant to him.

Arriving at the castle, she had to go through all the information again. Arguments broke out at the table everyone was seated around, none of them able to agree what they should do next.

Morgane rose from the table, placing her hands on it, looking at each of those seated there until they fell silent. "Two days. You all have two days to prepare and to gather allies. Then we attack." She strode from the room, Jorn and Becan following her.

Amber watched them leave. Two days. That'd give her enough time to help Ronan escape. And hopefully destroy the rest of the bracelets. She tried not to think of the ones in the tower room. Somehow they had to get rid of them too. And all the ones at the nest. She sighed heavily.

"What is wrong?" Treon, who was seated beside her, asked.

"There's still so much to do."

"Need a hand with anything?"

She shook her head, then nodded. "Yeah, you can help with the bracelets again." She might as well deal with a few more of them.

Chapter Twenty-Four

Treon took Amber to Brigitte's castle the next night so she could collect Ronan. It didn't take her long to find that he'd been moved to the same room that the bracelet's were stored in, either his bracelet active or wearing one Brigitte had placed on him. She stayed on Treon's back while he flew around the tower. Mentally searching the area, she drew in a quick breath.

"What did you discover?"

She didn't answer him. Had no idea if she should let anyone know there was an egg in the tower room. An egg that she was pretty certain contained two hatchlings. She really needed to be closer to know for certain and to tell if they were Gold. "I can't get him out. There are too many warriors in the room with him."

"What do you want to do?" Treon did another lap around the tower.

Amber wanted to tell him to attack, or create a diversion, but she didn't. "Take me back to your parents' castle." They had a battle to face tomorrow. The hunter was the priority. Ronan could wait. Hopefully. Surely Brigitte wouldn't kill him if she was keeping him in the room with the egg.

"Are you certain?"

She wasn't at all certain about anything. "Yeah. We can't do anything until after we deal with the hunter." She tried not to think about all the things that could go wrong. There were far too many of them. And she was still thinking of them when she went to sleep that night, her dreams disturbed by visions of Ronan's tortured body, Brigitte laughing manically as she killed him before coming after Amber.

Waking for what felt like the hundredth time, Amber climbed out of bed to stand at the window, looking at the grey light filling the sky. It would be time to go soon. A feeling shivered through her and she tried to figure out what it was. Fear. A smile formed. Ronan's predatory one. A very familiar fear. But this time it had been accompanied by a touch of excitement. She was about to take the first real step towards going home. Soon she'd see Kade. A fierce feeling raced through her, pushing away the fear. She was never going anywhere without her caged Pliethin again. In future, she'd sleep with it. Or maybe sleep with it on the floor beside the bed.

A light knock on the door had Amber facing it, having noticed Keeley walking along the corridor. She'd expected the hunter-dragon to walk past, not stop. "Yeah?"

Keeley opened the door. "I thought you were awake. Are you worried about the coming battle?"

Amber shrugged. "No more than usual."

Keeley grinned. "Join me for breakfast then. And we can compare battle stories."

She had no desire to talk about old battles, but breakfast sounded good. "Okay. I'll meet you in the dining room once I'm ready for the day." Or at least as ready as she was likely to be.

With a single nod, and another grin, Keeley closed the door and headed downstairs.

It didn't take Amber long to ready herself for the day and she joined Keeley at the table, surprised at how many were also there. The atmosphere was hushed and very few spoke, most of them talking quietly to the person next to them. Yet when it came time to prepare to leave, the noise grew as people argued, orders were given and final plans were made.

Like usual, Amber rode on Treon's back, wishing she not only had a saddle, but rode Kade instead. And had Crystal and Rian at her side. Probably Maira and Brann too. She missed everyone. Well, maybe not everyone. She hadn't thought once of Flinn. Or at least not until this moment.

"Are you all right?" Treon thought to Amber as they drew near to the nest.

"Yeah." She kept track of Brigitte's hunter. He was in the middle of the caves, very few around him. She didn't know if that was a good thing or not.

"Are you sure?" Treon bent the light around them. *"It's not too late–"*

She interrupted him. "I'm not about to let Brigitte's hunter escape."

Keeley flew in close to them. *"Are there many hunters at the nest?"*

Amber shook her head. "Only a couple. It's mostly wyverns and hybrids."

"Sounds like the type of battle people will talk about for centuries. That should make Cort happy." There was humour in Keeley's thoughts.

Amber assumed there was a joke, or something, that she was missing. "Only if we get Brigitte's hunter."

"Do you doubt we will?" Treon asked.

She wasn't about to share her fears with them. "I'll track him no matter where he goes." She saw the cave opening ahead of them, wyverns and hybrids pouring out of it. "Ignore the battle outside. The hunter is inside the cave."

"I wish I could go with you," Keeley thought to Amber and Treon. *"Without a hunter to keep me invisible I'll only give your position away."*

"We'll see you soon." Treon avoided the worst of the fighting, diving down to head in the cave.

"He's trying to leave," Amber warned him. "Keep going through the main part of the cave to a tunnel towards the rear on the left."

Treon followed Amber's directions, landing between the hunter and the tunnel entrance.

Amber scrambled off his back, throwing a fireball at the hunter who remained invisible even with her attack. The fireball seemed to hit a solid wall, being absorbed by it. She stared at the hunter she couldn't actually see. How was she meant to take him out? *"Go invisible, Treon and get behind him. I'll keep attacking him so you know where he is."* She threw fireballs at the hunter even though it did nothing to him.

The hunter became visible, a hooded, long sleeve shirt casting his face in shadows. "You waste your time."

Amber strode towards him, continuing to throw fireballs. "My time to waste." She kept her gaze on the hunter while she mentally tracked Treon. He was nearly in position.

Before Treon could come around behind the hunter, he spun and attacked, Treon unable to remain invisible. The hunter threw gusts of wind around, the strength of them pinning Treon to the ground.

Not knowing what to do, Amber ran at the hunter, daggers in hand.

He spun to face her, knocking her from her feet with a gust of wind, pinning her to the ground too. Laughing, he stood over her. "Do you know how many pathetic dragons and hunters try to kill me every year?"

"Why don't you tell me?" Amber found it hard to speak, the wind the hunter forced against her making it difficult to catch her breath.

"You'd think all of you would know how pointless it is by now." He stood over her.

Sensing Morgane, Jorn and Becan coming towards them, Amber smiled. "Without your magic, you'd be nothing."

"Power is all that matters." The hunter glanced in the direction Morgane and her companions came from. "You think I don't know when someone is coming after me? Even those who bend the light around themselves."

Her own words played over in her mind. Without your magic. The cold metal of the bracelets could be felt through her wrists sheaths. If only she could get close enough. Struggling against the wind, she half rose to her feet.

He threw another gust at her.

She met it with a fireball. The wind and fire collided, creating a sheet of fire that rose in swirls. She met his next gust the same way, noticing that he braced himself when her fireball collided with the wind. She quickly threw another fireball at the swirl of wind and fire. It exploded upwards and she threw herself at him, trying to tackle him to the ground.

He dragged her to the side with him when an arrow came for him, Morgane and her companions having arrived. He bent the light around them, hiding them from view and dragging Amber with him towards the tunnel.

Amber sent her thoughts to Treon, struggling against the hunter's grip. *"Block the tunnel."* She forced fireballs against the hunter's chest, grinning when he staggered. "Having problems?"

Treon landed in front of the tunnel.

The hunter looked between Amber and Treon. "You are in contact with him."

"You might say that." She sent an image to Morgane of exactly where the hunter was. An arrow came straight for him. While he was distracted trying to avoid the arrows, she unsnapped the bracelet and closed it over his wrist. Pain exploded through her when he drove what felt like a shard of ice through her side. A glance down showed it was exactly what it felt like.

The hunter pulled away from her and ran towards the front entrance.

Amber melted the ice, healing the wound as she ran after the hunter, showing Morgane where he was heading. Amber caught up with him as he spun to face her.

"How do you know where I am?" the hunter demanded.

Amber sent another image of where he was to Morgane, grabbing hold of the hunter's wrist as he tried to slip past her. She breathed Kade's name against the metal, the light no longer bending around the hunter.

"I have more than my power to fight with."

Amber sensed Treon, who was behind her, coming towards them, the rest of them closing in too.

"You've called hybrids." She raised her voice so that all those with her would know what was about to happen. She could sense at least twenty flying to the hunter's aid. They didn't have long. "The only problem is that they need to reach you in time."

The hunter drew a sword, knocking several arrows out of the air. "Seconds is all they need."

Amber's lips curved into a predatory smile. "I need less than that." She became a panther, leaping at the hunter, automatically going for his throat. He was dead before he hit the ground, hybrids surrounding them. *"We need to get out of here."* She thought the words to all of them with her, racing towards Treon who had bent the light around himself, as had Jorn and Cort who hid both themselves as well as Morgane and Becan.

"What about the bracelets that are being made?" Cort asked.

Amber, now in human form, had nearly reached Treon when a hybrid landed on her in wyvern form, pinning her to the ground. Pain shot through her as its claws sank into her flesh, making it impossible for her to answer.

"Take what you can. The only thing we needed to do was take out Brigitte's hunter and we've done that,"

Morgane thought to all of them. *"Organise those with us, Becan. Jorn and I will take care of this."*

Amber forced fireballs into the hybrid, fighting against the overwhelming pain. She heard rather than saw the arrows that thudded into the hybrid. Pain had the edges of her vision going black and for a second she could have sworn Kade was in the world. Fear rushed through her. She wasn't about to die here. Somehow she needed to find a way to rescue Ronan so they could go home.

The hybrid roared, his grip on her loosening.

It was enough for Amber to twist out of his grasp, her flesh tearing from the claws embedded in her. She'd barely taken two steps when Treon's arms wrapped around her, the light bending around the two of them as he dragged her to the side and away from the hybrid's attack.

"Heal yourself." Treon scooped her up, running towards the tunnel with her.

Behind them Amber sensed Morgane and her companions following, the hybrids erratically striking out at the air nearby. She drew power from several of her bracelets before healing herself, worried that if she'd attempted to heal herself without the power she might have passed out. Pain shot through her as Treon dashed to the side, colliding with a wall in an effort to avoid the random attacks from the hybrids. Again she thought she sensed Kade. And Rian. Her sense of them was gone as quickly as it came and she began to worry about how badly she was injured, trying to heal herself as Treon dodged the attacking hybrids.

Treon entered the tunnel, lowering her feet to the ground, keeping an arm around her waist to steady her. "It's too narrow for me to carry you." He pressed her against the wall, sheltering her with his body when several hybrids entered, having shifted to human form.

His warmth surrounded her, making her realise how cold she was. She stayed pressed against his chest until the hybrids had gone past, then stepped to the side. "I'm okay." She shivered at the loss of his warmth, realising she needed to heal herself further.

"Everyone is out of the caves. Some of them were able to take many of the bracelets," Treon said. "You ready to keep going?" He took a step in the direction the hybrids had taken.

She grabbed his arm, pulling him back towards her. "They're coming back this way. Two abreast. We need to get out of the tunnel. It'll be impossible for them to miss finding us."

Treon slipped his hand in hers, tugging her

towards the entrance of the tunnel. "We'll go through the main entrance." He paused a moment. "My parents asked if we need help."

"We're okay." Her body ached, her clothes were stained with blood and she was feeling more than a little exhausted. Yet her words felt true. Her gaze fell on the hunter as they walked past him, blood pooling around him. "We've weakened her." She stopped when once more she sensed Kade and this time Daray. "They're coming."

"Who is coming?" Treon looked over his shoulder. He tried to draw her in the direction of the entrance. "We have to get out of here."

A grin formed, excitement bursting through her. "They're coming!" She threw her arms around Treon, barely enclosing them around him before she was letting go and running towards the exit, keeping hold of his hand and tugging him along with her.

"What is going on?" Treon asked.

Stepping outside, Amber breathed in the cold air, the sharpness searing her lungs. But it didn't bother her. She was focused on what she could sense in the area where her and Ronan had first come into this world.

Treon shapeshifted. *"Hop on so we can get out of here."*

Amber clambered onto his back, tracking the movement of Kade, Rian, Crystal, Daray, Maira and Brann. They had found her. Or at least the world she was in. She couldn't stop grinning. They were in the direction of Morgane and Jorn's castle. "He came for me." Her words were soft, filled with excitement and wonder. "He came."

"Who came?" Treon flew towards his parents' castle.

"Kade." She could go home. Even thoughts of Ronan and Brigitte couldn't drown her excitement.

"Your dragon is in this world?"

Amber laughed at the confusion she could hear in Treon's thoughts. "Yes."

"You'll be going home."

She started to agree, her grin becoming the predatory smile instead. "I have a few things to do first." Ronan's wounds came to mind and the claw marks that had been on Keeley's face. "One thing in particular." She wasn't about to let Brigitte come after any of hers. And she would. After what they'd done to her today, she doubted Brigitte would rest until she'd destroyed each of them. Well, she wasn't about to let that happen.

Her hands tightened into fists, the fierce feeling filling her. No one would get away with going after those who were hers. Excitement mixed with the fierce feeling. She tracked Kade and those with him. Soon. She'd be with them soon. And then Brigitte would learn what happened to those who harmed her people. Ronan included. Because he was hers too. As much hers as she was his.

Free Ebook

Subscribe to Avril's newsletter and receive a free ebook. This ebook is exclusive to those on her mailing list. To find out more about this offer visit:

www.avrilsabine.com/free-ebook

*

We value your privacy and will not sell, rent, exchange or loan your email address to third parties. Your information is confidential and you are under no obligation to remain on the mailing list and can unsubscribe at any time.

Acknowledgements

As always, thanks to the usual crew and a special thanks to all those who emailed or messaged me about Amber, Kade and Ronan to tell me how much you enjoyed their story and asking for more.

To The Reader

If you enjoyed this book, why not consider leaving a review to help other readers discover it too? Reader engagement is one of the few ways that lets an author know readers want more books in a particular series or genre. So leave a review and tell friends, not only about this book but also about other ones you've enjoyed, so you can continue to enjoy books by your favourite authors for years to come.

Dreams are meant to be lived,

Avril.

About The Author

Avril is an Australian author who lives with her family on acreage in South East Queensland. She writes mostly young adult and children's speculative fiction, but has been known to dabble in other genres. You can find more information about her at www.avrilsabine.com where you can also subscribe to her newsletter to be kept informed about new releases, current projects, blog posts and exclusive news.

Titles By Avril Sabine

Stories about strong characters and characters who discover their strengths.

SERIES

Assassins Of The Dead- Young Adult Fantasy/ Paranormal

Book 1: Dark Blade

Book 2: Dragon Touched

Book 3: Society Against Vampires

Book 4: King's Request

Dragon Blood- Young Adult Urban Fantasy (with elements of romance)

(5 book series)

Book 1: Pliethin

Book 2: Wyvern

Book 3: Surety

Book 4: Knight

Book 5: Mage

Dragon Mage- Young Adult Urban Fantasy (with elements of romance)

(Series two of Dragon Blood series)

Book 1: Promise

Dragon Blood Chronicles- Young Adult Urban Fantasy (with elements of romance)

(Companion stand alone series to Dragon Blood)

Book 1: Oath

Book 2: Betrayed

Guardians Of The Round Table- Young Adult Fantasy LitRPG

(Co-written with Storm and Rhys Petersen)

Book 1: Dexterity Fail

Book 2: Goblin Boots

Book 3: Singed Feathers

Book 4: Frog Mage

Book 5: Crystal Mine

Book 6: Cursed Harp

Rosie's Rangers- Young Adult Western Steampunk

(6 book series)

Book 1: Justice

Book 2: Vengeance

Book 3: Treachery

Book 4: Accused

Book 5: Wanted

Book 6: Corruption

Mark Of Kings- Children's Fantasy

(Upper middle grade/preteen)

(4 book series)

Book 1: The Arena

Book 2: The Island

Book 3: The Assassin

Book 4: The King

STAND ALONE SERIES

Demon Hunters- Young Adult Urban Fantasy/ Horror (with elements of romance)

Book 1: Blood Sacrifice

Book 2: Retribution

Book 3: Tainted

Book 4: Premonition

Book 5: Cursed

Book 6: Feud

Book 7: Extrication

Plea Of The Damned- Young Adult Urban Fantasy/Paranormal

(6 book series)

Book 1: Forgive Me Lucy

Book 2: Forgive Me Aiden

Book 3: Forgive Me Jena

Book 4: Forgive Me Kobe

Book 5: Forgive Me Marti

Book 6: Forgive Me Dawson

Realms Of The Fae- Young Adult Urban Fantasy (with elements of romance)

The Sword (short story in Like A Girl Anthology)

Heart Of Stone

Book 1: A Debt Owed

Book 2: Marked By The Hunt

Book 3: The Magic Collector

Book 4: An Unexpected Betrayal

Book 5: Imprisoned By Iron

Fairytales Retold (Short Stories)

Snow-White And Rose-Red

The Twelve Brothers

The Light Princess

Beauty And The Beast

Sleeping Beauty

Aschenputtel

The Golden Bird

The Frog Prince

The Death Of Koshchei The Deathless

Myths And Legends Retold (Short Stories)

Ion, Son Of Apollo

Sir Gawain And The Maid With The Narrow Sleeves

Princess Ilse, The Giant's Daughter

YOUNG ADULT NOVELS

Young Adult Fantasy (with elements of romance)

Elf Sight

Earth Bound

Young Adult Urban Fantasy

Stone Warrior (with elements of romance)

The Jungle Inside

Young Adult Contemporary (with elements of romance)

Through Your Eyes

The Ugly Stepsister

Perfect Little Princess

Young Adult Contemporary/Paranormal

Whispers In The Dark (with elements of romance and same sex relationships)

Over Too Soon (with elements of romance)

Young Adult Sci-Fi

Experiment X-One-Six (Urban Sci-Fi/Superheroes)

An Endless Dawn (Post Apocalyptic Sci-Fi)

CHILDREN'S BOOKS

Dragon Lord (Preteen/early teens) (Fantasy)

The Irish Wizard (Upper middle grade) (Urban Fantasy)

SHORT STORIES

Urban Fantasy

Eternally Late

Dealings With Joe

Glimpses (short story in That Moment When Anthology)

Contemporary

The Brat Next Door

Fantasy LitRPG

(Set in the same world as Guardians Of The Round Table Series)

Tales Of Inadon 1: The Disc (Co-written with Storm and Rhys Petersen) (short story in Game On! Anthology)

Post Apocalyptic Sci-Fi

Compulsive Directive

NONFICTION

A Year Of Weekly Writing Exercises (Creative Writing)

Cooking For Families With Allergies (Cooking) (Co-written with Storm Petersen)

Tell Me A Story, Grandma (Memoir)

For the most up to date details on available titles visit:

www.avrilsabine.com/books/bibliography

Dragon Mage Series

To learn more about this series visit:

www.avrilsabine.com/series/db

BOOKS AVAILABLE IN THE DRAGON MAGE SERIES

(Series two of Dragon Blood series)

Book 1: Promise

BOOKS SET BEFORE THE DRAGON MAGE SERIES

Dragon Blood

(5 book series)

Book 1: Pliethin

Book 2: Wyvern

Book 3: Surety

Book 4: Knight

Book 5: Mage

BOOKS SET IN THE SAME WORLD AS THE
DRAGON MAGE SERIES

Dragon Blood Chronicles

(Companion stand alone series to Dragon Blood)

Book 1: Oath

Book 2: Betrayed (Set before Dragon Blood Series)

Disclaimer

This is a work of fiction. Names, characters, businesses, places, events and incidents are either the products of the author's imagination or used in a fictitious manner. Any resemblance to actual persons, living or dead, or actual events is purely coincidental. The opinions expressed or beliefs held are those of the characters and should not be assumed to be the opinions or beliefs of the author.